Little Rabbit

Little Rabbit

ALYSSA SONGSIRIDEJ

BLOOMSBURY PUBLISHING
NEW YORK · LONDON · OXFORD · NEW DELHI · SYDNEY

BLOOMSBURY PUBLISHING
Bloomsbury Publishing Inc.
1385 Broadway, New York, NY 10018, USA

BLOOMSBURY, BLOOMSBURY PUBLISHING, and the Diana logo
are trademarks of Bloomsbury Publishing Plc

First published in the United States 2022

ISBN: HB: 978-1-63557-869-0; EBOOK: 978-1-63557-870-6

Library of Congress Cataloging-in-Publication Data is available

2 4 6 8 10 9 7 5 3 1

Typeset by Westchester Publishing Services
Printed and bound in the U.S.A.

To find out more about our authors and books visit
www.bloomsbury.com and sign up for our newsletters.

Bloomsbury books may be purchased for business or promotional use. For
information on bulk purchases please contact Macmillan Corporate and
Premium Sales Department at specialmarkets@macmillan.com.

For Matt

CHAPTER ONE

S he wore the same outfit as all the other dancers onstage, a plain leotard cut to show muscle flexed tight around bone. But unlike the others, she wore her hair loose and swinging, and that's how I knew she was special, a lead.

I'd bought a ticket to the performance even though I didn't know anything about dance. But I knew the director of the company, the choreographer. We'd been at a residency together in the North Woods of Maine, where I'd finished the edits for my first book. But I didn't know him well, hadn't talked to him much. He'd annoyed me, dominating dinner with stories about his dance career, about becoming a choreographer. "I'm not good at being someone else's puppet," he would say. "I'm better at running the show."

So I was surprised when, a little less than a year after our time together, he emailed to say his company was coming up to do a few shows in Boston. It'd be nice if I could make it, he wrote. To catch up.

I didn't reply, but still I bought the cheapest ticket and caught the crowded T after work, ferried over the river into the glass and lights of the city. Leaving the station, I crossed the dark Common and searched for the right spot in the bright bowels of the theater district.

Slipping into the back of the auditorium, I expected to be confused, to not understand. I hadn't expected to be hollowed out and gutted, watching the long-haired dancer swirling in the middle of the others. The surrounding performers stayed small and muted, offsetting her dynamic turns and leaps. Her spine curved, all coiled power, bright energy spitting from her fingers, her hips, and added feet.

The pit of my stomach pulled up to my ribs, following her, reacting. Watching her taught me something I would need years to learn how to say. *We're alone in a body*, I thought. Our forms are hollow shells until our souls came to fill them. Then we bumbled, lost to each other, separate and apart.

After the performance, I moved with the crowd to leave, but then I saw the choreographer. He stood alone, watching the flow of spectators drifting toward the door. Straight-backed, alert, his training and discipline marked his body even when he thought he was alone. He wore his black clothing like camouflage, the beauty almost hidden until your attention engaged. Then the noticing, the understanding, the elegance emerging from the build of his bones.

I cut across the flow of people toward him. When he first saw me, his face didn't react, my identity failing to register. I panicked. Maybe he wouldn't remember me, and I'd look like a fool.

But then his expression broke into recognition. He smiled and hugged me so lightly his arms barely pressed down on my puffy coat.

"You didn't reply to my email," he said. "I thought maybe you'd moved. That you wouldn't come."

"Sorry, I forgot," I said. "It was wonderful, thanks for inviting me."

His attention locked on me, letting go of the other people in the room. He kept brushing his hair back. "What have you been up to," he asked, "since Maine?"

"Working," I said. "What about you?"

"We just wrapped a European tour."

Standing in the stark, modern theater lobby, I began to feel irradiated by his in-the-world glamour, a different him from the one at the rural residency. He looked right in that space, austere and clean. With him, I began to feel like the wrong species of animal, all slump-backed and shabby.

I didn't have much time to feel awkward, though. Behind him, a hidden door cracked open and the dancers slipped out, washed and freshly clothed.

"Wonderful," he said, stepping aside to let us face one another. "I'd like to introduce you." He told them my name, how we knew each other, Maine. "A wonderful writer," he said, and I grew hot. "But she was always running off to work. Our nickname for her was 'Little Rabbit.'"

I felt annoyed all over again. Why did he have to tell them that? Maybe coming by was a mistake.

The lead dancer stood at the back of the group, her long hair spilling over the shoulders of her faux leather coat. *She's going to freeze*, I thought. A streak of bright metallic bronzer highlighted the slope of her cheeks.

"Are you going to come out with us?" one of the male dancers asked the choreographer.

"No," he said. He gestured to me. "We need to catch up."

Usually I would have refused. I woke up at five A.M. every day to write before going to my office job. But I wanted to follow him. Maybe I wanted some of that glamour, or to at least slip back into the brief time at the residency when writing had been my life.

The freezing wind cut through even my puffy coat, so we picked the first place we passed, a bland, corporate hotel bar. White subway tiles, brass fixtures, the other patrons emitting a kind of ambient aggression.

The hostess put us next to the window at a small, round table cut from veined marble. I cradled the cocktail menu with jittery hands. I'd never been alone with the choreographer before. I couldn't think of anything to say.

He spoke first. "I read your book," he said.

"Really?" My book had been published by my friend's small press, the last they published before suddenly folding. Half of the edition of five hundred sat in the distributor's warehouse, and the other half was in my bedroom closet.

"Yes," he said. "I thought it was great. Really different. Does that make sense?"

"Lots of people have called it different."

"Sorry—I wish I could talk about it better," he said. "It's really impressive to me, to work in words. It seems difficult. To take the thing we all use every day and try to make it art."

"Yeah," I said, flipping a menu page, "it really sucks."

The waiter came to take our drink order. I'd barely read the options. "Do you have Talisker?" I asked.

"Yes, Miss."

"I'll have that, neat."

"And you, sir?"

"A gin martini." He handed the menu on.

Our shields were gone. There was nothing to look at except each other.

I knew, right then, that I would sleep with him. A flash of lightning down my lower spine, knowledge but also a question. Maybe not that night. But knowing sparked the space between us, turning it electric so I became uncomfortably aware of the distance between our knees.

"And what did you think of the performance?" he asked.

"Great," I said. I remembered the lead dancer with her long, swinging hair. "Sorry, I really don't know anything about dance."

"Even better," he said, leaning forward on his elbows. "I love hearing impressions from people who aren't in my world."

His smooth skin seemed ready to tip into weathered, his dark hair shot full of gray. Solidly middle aged.

The waiter brought over our drinks, giving me time to choose my words. "I guess I found it frightening," I said. "It made me feel alone. In my body."

I sipped my Scotch, forcing my gaze down at the table so I wouldn't study his reaction. "Good," he said.

I put the glass down, already woozy. "I think I need to order some food," I said. "Or I'm going to end up drunk."

I ordered a cheeseburger topped with mushrooms, and he picked the kale salad. I'd forgotten that he was vegan. "You know," he said, "I got the impression that you didn't like me very much, when we were in Maine."

"You did?" I swallowed a bite of meat and tried to dab the grease delicately with my napkin.

"Why was that?"

"You talked too much," I explained. "At dinner."

He stabbed a kale leaf. "Dinner is for talking."

"Not only you, though."

The kale leaves disappeared. He seemed capable of eating without visibly crunching or chewing. "Point taken," he said. "I'm sorry."

I finished my Talisker. Maybe I would order another. "Why did you invite me, then, if you didn't like me," I said.

"I only said that you didn't like me."

I stuck my chin forward. Insolent. Suggestive. "So you do like me."

His expression remained controlled, taking in the boldness on my face. "Yes," he said. "I like you quite a lot."

He wrote down his number on a scrap of paper before I got in my rideshare, in case I ever came to New York. Then he hugged me, just my arms and shoulders.

I kept the paper in my left hand, the phone in my right as the car weaved and turned along the road beside the river. Something rushed along inside me, a movement that felt like certainty, and finally I entered the number into my phone for safekeeping.

CHAPTER TWO

The question of sleeping with the choreographer, of what it would feel like to touch him, knocked around inside of me until winter broke into rainy New England spring. Finally, I came up with an excuse. I convinced a friend at a small cultural magazine to let me profile the choreographer and his dance company. No one would pay me, and I'd have to buy my own train ticket and stay on my friend's couch in Sunset Park, but it gave me a reason to email him that I was coming.

Good, he wrote back. *You can stop in on a rehearsal.*

At some point during the train ride down the coast, the cool spring switched to sudden muggy presummer, a bubble of heat and humidity that only grew overnight as I sweated and turned on my friend's stiff foldout couch. The heat dampened my anticipation, muddling my expectations with my own gross humanity.

I had to take three different trains to get to the choreographer's rehearsal space, and during the journey I absorbed vast quantities of the city's grime and dirt. By the time I got to the school turned performing arts studio, I'd sweated through my linen blouse, my denim shorts, transformed into a swamp of a human being.

The cool walls of the old brownstone building mixed with the heat so the air turned strange and clammy. Walking through the long halls of identical doors, I felt like a child again, suddenly oversize, wandering until I found the sounds of music and counting.

I could hear his voice, the sound of his hands clapping. Wiping my sweaty palms on my shorts, I grabbed the door handle and pulled.

The rehearsal space still felt like a classroom, the walls a different color where the chalkboards had been. Cool air rattled through new aluminum vents. Six or seven glorious bodies moved through the middle of the room, cutting around each other, stopping, stretching, lifting and throwing one dancer to another. Even though I'd never seen anyone else do the things they did, their bending, twisting feats made them seem more human, like they'd found new doors into how to be a body.

The choreographer stood in front of them all, watching them, instructing. He wore a white T-shirt, soft black pants, his arms wrapped around his torso as he focused. I could see the line of his waist, the lean muscles that still bound him. "More point with the chin," he called. "You should be leading with the sternum. Carry the motion through."

I closed the door silently behind me, but he still noticed and walked over. "Could you take off your shoes?" he asked, looking at my dirty white sneakers. A soft, matte material covered the oddly springy floor.

"Sorry," I said, toeing them off.

"They changed as soon as you walked in the door," he said, looking at the dancers. "Just a millimeter tighter."

"I'm sorry," I repeated.

"No, it's the permanent problem of a performer," he said. "It's just too bad you'll never see how they move when we're alone."

He went back to his spot, watching the dancers and shouting out commands, suggestions so specific I couldn't follow. The song ended, the performers hitting their last pose. "Good work," he said, clapping. "Now let's get Jackie, TJ, and Zac for the trio."

Jackie was the dancer with the long brown hair. Today she'd wrapped it up in a tight ballerina bun and dressed her body in a white leotard made of tissue-thin fabric. I stared at the muscles winging across her back, her thighs, until I felt absurd, goggle-eyed.

She turned away from my gaze, her forearms up against the back of her head with her mouth pressed into her bicep. Her right leg was up, and the two male dancers crowded the floor around her, one taking her raised calf in his palm. They held still for a beat, turned into living Grecian statues.

Then the music began and they sprang to life, one male dancer lifting Jackie, their backs to each other, then tossing her to the other who caught her by the waist. She seemed trapped for a moment with her leg stiff behind her before swirling free, the world turned by her hips.

"Stop," the choreographer called. "Jackie, you need to be initiating the movement more from the pelvic bowl." He crossed the room to stand next to her, pointing his thumbs at his own hips. "Imagine you have two strings tugging your iliac crests." He swiveled to demonstrate, shifting the balance of his knees. Jackie copied him. I reached into my leather satchel for water, but I didn't have any. I felt a pen. Oh notes, I remembered. I should be taking notes.

"And when you hit the right elbow—hit it." She struck a pose with her right elbow up and out. "You need to point a little higher." He touched her elbow with two fingers, adjusting. "And look a little more this way." The fingers went to her cheek, guiding her face. "So you're looking stage left. Right there. Right at her." They locked on me, the choreographer pointing. Jackie smiled, and I gave a small, stupid wave.

Once rehearsal finished, the dancers fell upon their bags, gathering their empty Tupperware, their water bottles, as they reassembled their outside selves. I stood in the corner, watching everyone leave. "Good work," the choreographer said. "See you Wednesday." The last one—TJ?—left, and then the chore-ographer and I were alone.

He stood by the door at the opposite end of the room. "Shall we?"

The choreographer lived only a short train ride away. Shoved into the full subway car, I hung heavily on the metal bar. The jolts and stops swayed me toward him, each drift sending a light shock through my body.

I still didn't say anything as I followed him up the stairs into his building, stepping into a comfortable two-bedroom apart-ment with an open common area and plush suede couches. The windows looked out onto trees, the street. Almost every other New York apartment I'd been in looked out on an airshaft.

"Do you want a day drink?" he asked me.

"What's in a day drink?" I said. I didn't look at him, pretending to study his prints, the books on his shelves.

"Like, a spritz." He stepped behind the granite counter into the kitchen area.

I rubbed the back of my neck, feeling the grit and slime on my skin. "Actually, could I take a shower?" I asked.

He paused, holding a bottle of Aperol. "Sure," he said. "There's extra towels by the sink."

I meant to just rinse off, but the bottles lining the frosted window ledge looked gender-neutral and expensive. I flipped the cap off one and sniffed. It smelled deeply herbaceous, like thyme. I rubbed the foam through my hair, his soap on my skin.

After I'd cleaned up, fresh and new, I didn't know what else to do but put the clothes I'd come in back on, the fabric still soiled with my own sweat.

He'd fixed the drinks while I was in the bathroom, and his forearms flexed as he screwed the cap back on the Aperol. I just wanted to watch him. The light from the window turned his shirt translucent, his lean muscles visible as shadows under the fabric. Rarely had I been so close to such gorgeous masculinity.

He looked at me, my wet hair dripping dark spots onto my shirt. "The drinks are ready," he said, picking up both glasses. Our fingers brushed as I took mine, warm flesh on cold glass.

"Do you feel better, after your shower?" he asked. We stood, even though there was ample seating.

"My clothes still feel dirty," I said. The air pulsed, turning thick like it would keep us apart.

"That's unfortunate," he said.

The drinks stood between us, stupidly in our hands. "I don't want a drink," I said, putting it down on the table.

"No?" he said. I stepped toward him and he leaned back. But I also saw the glass leave his hand, slipped out onto the table.

He froze, I froze him, so I came right up but still didn't touch, holding just at the edge. "Maybe I shouldn't have gotten dressed," I said.

His hands took me around my ribs, as if to brace me and keep me away. I flushed, the heat of first touch.

"Is this what you want?" he asked, the magnetic pull of my body defying his push so I ended up right against him, my hands resting on his chest before sliding to his neck. He felt firm underneath his thin clothing, all potential and power.

"Why do you think I came here?" I said, and then I stretched my spine so I could reach him, kiss him, his mouth taking its time to respond, first slow and still before turning fluid and open and pressing.

I removed the shirt I'd just put back on, the bra, the shorts, disrobing fully there beside his dining room table. I pulled off his shirt, his pants. "Slow down," he said, but I wouldn't. I would take what I'd come for.

Bare, I wrapped my arms around his neck and pressed my length against him, my softness melting around his hard. His height meant our bodies didn't match, standing like that, his hip points pressed into me. *Iliac crests.* I'd wrapped my thumbs around the curved bones. I'd kiss them, expose them.

His body resisted, a wall against me and what I wanted even though it was the thing I'd come to take. He kept his touch light, all that strength held back by internal restraint. "Are you sure this is what you want?" he asked again as he guided me toward the darkened bedroom.

"Do you need me to convince you?" I asked.

And then I was on my back, looking up at him, at the expanse of his chest and the articulation of his neck. My knees pulled up obediently as his hand pushed between my legs, looking for evidence. I gasped, surprised as his fingers found the right places.

My own hands reached for him in turn, cupping and stroking, kissing and biting whatever part of his flesh became available, until I finally felt that dam inside him relent, his own hunger pouring over me.

By the time we got to the drinks, the ice had melted. He threw them out, mixed some more, and brought them into bed. I felt parched, wrung out, swallowing greedily even though alcohol wasn't the solution.

"Do you come to New York often?" he asked.

"No," I said. "The train's kind of expensive."

He sat on top of the covers. Just lounging in bed, he still had good posture, like he'd been drawn with only straight lines.

"What about the Berkshires?" he asked.

"What about the Berkshires?" I repeated.

"I have a house up there. Good hiking."

I looked down at the perfect square cubes in my glass. "How do you afford this?" I asked. "I know you're doing really well. But this . . . It seems like a lot."

He sipped his drink. "My ex-wife was a very rich woman," he said. "She liked to invest. Me, my company, my career—all investments."

"She didn't want to take anything with her?"

"She took some things," he said. "But she left me for a man even richer than her, so she let me have what I wanted."

I stuck my thumbnail into one of the lines etched in the crystal glass. "That's nice," I said. "Did you love her?"

"I admire her."

"Did she love you?"

"She finds me interesting," he said. "She's actually still a donor."

"Even nicer," I said. The information zipped between us, taking up air. "And no kids." They were always obvious, the ones at the residency without kids.

"No."

"Parents?"

"Dead. I have a younger sister," he said.

"I have an older brother."

He laughed. "Oh god. If my sister slept with someone that much older than her."

Time to drain my drink. I knocked the sweet, bitter liquid back. "I don't often call my brother to tell him who I'm sleeping with," I said as the cubes landed at the bottom of the glass.

He dropped his head, trying to look at me from a different angle. "Please tell me you're in your thirties," he said.

"I'm thir-*ty*."

He laughed, but also groaned, then reached over and took my glass. I watched him walk naked to the kitchen to refill it. "And you're from Pennsylvania," he said from the other room. "I remember from your book."

My editor, really my friend, had tried to sell my book as a "fragmentary hallucination." It took place in a Central PA town haunted from below by demon-ghosts that were also, somehow, capitalism.

"Yep," I said. "My parents still live there."

He handed over my fresh drink. I suddenly felt very naked. My hair had dried and smelled like plants. "My friend's place is a long train ride away," I began.

"You can stay here," he said. "I'll give you some clothes to wear."

And he got up to refill his drink before he'd even finished it.

I WOKE DISORIENTED, not in my bed, his sleeping hand still gripped around my hip. I pulled away, sitting up to look at him in the morning light. He'd slept on his side, his lovely face smooshed and drooping.

"Are you just going to stare at me?" he said, his eyes still closed.

"How old are you?" I asked.

He opened his eyes and sat up, using his fingers to rub life and flexibility back into his expression. "I'm fifty-one," he said. "I'm guessing right now I look it."

I turned away so as not to confirm anything.

"What are you thinking?" he asked.

I took a full breath before answering. "That I've checked off a new box."

My phone on the nightstand buzzed. Probably Rita, the friend I was supposed to be staying with, texting sexually suggestive emojis. I turned to get it, but he grabbed my wrist, the solidity of his grip startling.

"Where are you going," he said, but he wasn't asking a question.

He rolled himself above but not on me, his body suspended as his hands slid under my pelvis, scooping. My body lost its rigidity, my center dropping into my hips.

"You'll tell me if something's not okay, Rabbit," he said, tugging down my cotton pants. His cotton pants.

"I don't think that name fits," I said, but my voice was gasping. I turned away to stare up at the ceiling, as if the force of looking could anchor me. "I'm not cute."

"Bunnies are cute," he said, kissing my knees. He found the tender spot of my inner thighs, brushing it with his mouth so I gasped again. "Rabbits are small and wild and determined to survive."

Now my eyes were shut. His fingers slipped inside me again, finding what he needed in order to take me. "Tell me what you like," I said.

He moved above me, his other hand reaching for my open mouth so he could slide his fingers over the wet muscle of my tongue. "Darling," he said as he began to work, "I can't wait to teach you."

CHAPTER THREE

I stayed at the choreographer's so late I had to take a ride-share to my friend's place, grab my stuff, then immediately get another rideshare to Penn Station where I almost missed my train.

We pulled into Boston a few hours later. Another rideshare back to my apartment in Somerville, where Annie's bedroom door stood open, her lamp shining through to the kitchen. "Hello, my life," she called.

I dropped my bags, my key clattering on the mail table. "What? What life?" I called back, the quote as familiar in my mouth as hello. "No life of mine." Our little game, ever since our first semester of college, when Annie stopped me at a campus reading and demanded to know my name. Instead of doing our homework, we'd lounge on each other's extra-long twins or the warm campus lawn, reading our favorite short stories out loud. Annie wrote, too. But she had an agent who sent her work off to the fancy magazines and a day job at a big literary nonprofit downtown. Online, a sleek and glamorous

Annie posed with famous authors in lavish Back Bay mansions, glass of wine in hand.

She shuffled out of her room in tattered slippers, cotton shorts, and a Wellesley sweatshirt, her long blonde hair pulled up in a messy puff. "How was the train ride?" she asked.

"Fine." I left my bags by the door to be dealt with later. Our apartment smelled like old wood and paint and Annie's coconut lotion. Usually, the odor comforted me.

"What did I miss?" I asked, getting a glass of water. I poured from the tap and drank. I kept on drinking. I couldn't get enough.

"I had dinner with Tia and Elle. Elle's really thinking about grad school."

"That's great," I said.

"Yeah, but Tia's upset, because they're looking outside of Boston."

I got more water. "But there's a million schools in Boston."

"That's what I said."

Annie talked on about the food, the drinks, going out to Revere Beach with our friends to watch the seagulls devour the plentiful surf clams. I only half listened, letting the details filter through me.

"And how was New York?" Annie asked. "What'd you think of the Judy Chicago exhibit?"

Annie, a great lover of itineraries, had given me a list of things to do, food to eat and an absolute order that I go to the Brooklyn Museum. "I didn't make it," I admitted. I opened the fridge. Maybe food would help. I felt emptied and rattled, like I needed settling.

"Oh no," Annie said. I'd been enthusiastic about the suggestion. "What happened?"

I hadn't told Annie about the choreographer. Unusual, but I noticed only now that the fact had passed. "I met up with someone. From that residency I went to?" I picked up a block of pale grocery store cheese. Circles of bluish mold had sprouted across the end. "And we, ah, hooked up."

"Really?" Her body pulled closer to mine out of curiosity.

"Yeah. I ended up staying with him."

She followed me around the kitchen. "A him?" she repeated. "Like a cis him?"

"Yep." I brought the cheese to the counter, cutting off the mold.

Annie's hands rested on the edge near the cutting board. She'd repainted her nails with my polish, a creamy cement color. "I can't remember the last time you slept with a man."

"I can," I said, "unfortunately."

She took one of my clean cheese slices, nibbling on the end. "How'd it go with this one?"

I felt the choreographer's hands on my bare thighs as he lifted me against the counter, the wall. My cries so loud he stopped to shush me, laughing. *You're going to bring the neighbors.*

"Fine," I said.

She stepped close, lifting my hair to expose my beet-red ears. "Oh my god, you're blushing."

"Stop it," I said, pushing her hand back.

"Wait, was this the dance guy?" she said. She knew about the show in Boston. "I knew something was up. You don't know anything about dance."

"I like to learn things."

"I bet you do." Her voice turned gravelly with suggestion.

"Stop it." I finished the cheese and put the plate in the sink. "It went well. It was a nice time."

I blasted the faucet to wash away the crumbs. Annie watched. I knew the crook of her mouth, the lines of skepticism. She'd pursue me, tease me if she felt me holding back.

"You stayed at his apartment," she said. "A stranger?"

"He wasn't a stranger," I said. I started scrubbing the plate now with the all-natural brush Annie liked, the nontoxic dish soap that didn't quite foam. "I told you, we met at that residency."

"What did you guys do?" she asked.

I felt his chest under my hand, the press of his breathing against me. Overwhelmed, I pulled myself back into the kitchen, focusing on the cool tile under my feet. Home with Annie, back in my life.

"Nothing," I said. "I don't feel like talking about it."

"Okay, okay," Annie said, giving in. She hugged me from behind, her head on my shoulder. "Sorry to bug you. You had fun, though, right?"

I put the plate in the dish rack with all the other plates Annie had failed to put away. "Yeah, I did," I said drying my hands. *Fun.* The word felt small and casual, light.

She let me go. "Do you think you'll see him again?"

I placed my hands on the back of my neck to warm them. "He lives in New York," I said. But I saw the Berkshires, the mountains just on the other end of the Mass Pike.

"Right," Annie said. She hugged me from the side with one arm, her hair fragrant with fruity shampoo. "Not exactly local."

I leaned back, letting her body take some of my balance and weight. "Nope," I said. "Have you had dinner?"

"No. Want to order from Himalayan Kitchen?"

"Yes, please." I tugged my hair out of my bun, releasing a whiff of the choreographer's shampoo. "I'm going to take a shower. Can you order my usual?"

I made the water hot, scrubbing off the train, the choreographer on my skin. But I could still feel the heat of his hands all over me.

I got into my own slouchy at-home clothes and joined Annie on the couch with the takeout, both of us eating straight from the containers. We curled our legs up underneath us, bare knees and feet pointed in different directions.

We tried to watch *The Handmaid's Tale* on Annie's laptop, but there were too many references to Somerville. "I feel really depressed," I said, biting into the hot chili crust of my spicy *momo*. "Could we switch to *Frances Ha*?"

"Whatever milady desires," Annie said, putting down the container and reaching for the computer.

I watched Greta Gerwig's lanky form dip and stretch. The dancers at rehearsal. Jackie.

My phone on the coffee table buzzed. I put down the food and checked the message. *Rabbit*, it said, *Did you get home safe?*

"I don't like it when she goes to Japan," Annie said, struggling to keep hold of the *momo* with the splintery takeout chopsticks. "Can we just skip to the end?"

I reached for the top of the takeout container, closing it back up. "Actually, I think I need to go to sleep," I said, standing and stretching.

"Alright," Annie said. She stopped the movie with her toe, putting the empty *momo* container down. "Glad you're back." She smiled at me.

"Me too," I said.

Annie stayed on the couch, checking her email. I made sure to close my bedroom door.

Alone, standing in the middle of my room, I looked at the message again. *Yes, back*, I replied, then added, *Thx for the weekend*, before throwing the phone on my bed.

I RETURNED TO Boston expecting to have been inoculated against the choreographer, the shot of sexual experience protecting me from further occupation. But I wasn't done. In the boring moments of my job, of which there were many, my imagination fell into bed with him, wrapped in an expert body both attentive and withholding. As I walked back and forth from work, each step turned into a question. The way he'd moved and touched me felt controlled by a careful force. What stood on the other side of it? My body wanted to know the answer.

And so I felt a ping of thrill when my phone buzzed with a fresh email from him.

Rabbit,

I saw a film last night that made me think of you. The Umbrellas of Cherbourg. *I have no idea why you came to mind—it's a goddamn musical. Maybe I just imagine that it rains a lot in Boston.*

But I wanted to know if you had seen it, wanted to talk to you about it. Which is a way of saying that I'd like to see you again.

Have you thought more about the Berkshires?

He signed off with his first initial.

The phone now had an extra weight and warmth, a spare life in my pocket. It held the email, the pleasure of being pursued. I kept myself from writing back for as long as I could stand it.

Yes, I've seen it, I wrote. *I love it, but also think it's weird that it made you think of me. My sunny tragedy? I imagine it's not because of Catherine Deneuve.*

The Berkshires has crossed my mind. Do you ever come to Boston first?

After work, I walked back through Cambridge up the hill into Somerville, passing the grand houses with their luscious, fenced-in gardens. Lilacs in full bloom, hedges of heady, fragrant cones. I remembered that he loved them, the flowers and their smell. I didn't know why I had that information. He must have said something about it in Maine.

By the time I reached my apartment, I had another email from him. No greeting, just—*I don't come to Boston, but I can.*

His intent circled me like an animal.

After dinner, I sent back my own spare reply. *I'm free the weekend after next.* Then followed up: *But warning, I have a roommate.*

I vacuumed, cleaned—for the first time ever, Annie accused—then I went to the drugstore and bought condoms. I hadn't bought them in quite a long time—my last partner had been a judgmental white lesbian named Peggy—and so I'd forgotten the awkwardness of it, what count was appropriate. Then I had to face a human being with my decision because the self-checkout was broken. At home, I hid the box in my nightstand drawer. What absurd little objects.

The choreographer called when he was outside so I could come down and bring him the visitor parking pass. He waited by the open driver's side door, his long arms resting on the window. For a moment, I watched him, his eyes scanning the perimeter like a wary animal.

As soon as he saw me, his limbs lifted and straightened, coming to life. He pulled his sunglasses off his head, brushed his hair. "Hi," I said, holding out the parking pass. I kept two arms' lengths between us.

He put the pass on the dashboard, then caught my torso, his arms longer than I'd thought. "Hello," he said, pulling me in and kissing me lightly on the mouth. "Nice neighborhood."

I felt stunned by the kiss. I thought, *We're in public*, as if it were a crime. "Do you want to go for a walk?" I asked.

"No thanks."

As we got closer to my apartment, I grew embarrassed in advance. Annie and I had lived in the place for three years. We'd tried to make it cute with secondhand furniture and mismatched cookware, but the apartment had never stopped feeling temporary. Everything cheap, disposable, except for whatever Annie's mother brought over.

But he didn't look at anything in the common area. Not the IKEA butcher-block counter or Annie's Le Creuset. "Which one's yours?" he asked, glancing at the bedrooms at opposite ends of the apartment.

"That one," I said, pointing to my open door. I'd tidied up, made my bed, but when he walked in, everything I'd picked to decorate my life looked young and expendable. His bag was simple but well made, costly. I hated that I kept on noticing his things.

He sat on the end of my bed and looked at me, his gaze thick, physical. I stood by the door, tense and held back.

"Come here," he said.

My skin felt like an independent creature, all awake with expectation. I shut the door and took my time walking over to him, then eased myself onto his lap. Wrapping my hands around his head, I pulled his mouth up, kissing. His hands took command of my torso, my ribs, cupping them lightly as if the bones were easy to break. He still touched me with a strange care, like folding something delicate.

I peeled his shirt off, fanning my fingers across the muscles of his shoulders as he pressed his face into the knit of my ribs. *Beauty*, I thought, breathing in.

Then I pushed him down onto his back and pulled off my dress. He grabbed my torso again, laughing as he shifted me over him. "You're always in such a big hurry," he said, unhooking my bra.

I kept my mouth on him, my hand sliding down between his legs. He groaned, grabbed my wrist. "Slow down," he said, but he didn't move my arm, allowing me to keep working him.

He took off my underwear and I got up long enough to remove his pants, pausing to look at him on my bed. He looked all wrong there, like I'd stolen a work of art and brought it back to my room.

His hands found me before I expected it, his fingers driving up inside. My hips bucked, a shock of pleasure spiraling up my spine. Then he prepped me until the time was right and pulled me over and onto him.

He finished before I wanted him to. I got off, laid down on my stomach and watched his breathing slow until the pace had returned to normal.

"I know you're not done," he said, his hand in my hair.

"I can finish."

"No," he said. His fingers pressed into my cheek. "Just give me a minute."

All wound up, I watched him gather himself, his eyes closed as he performed some deep breathing exercise. Then a thought brought him out of the moment, making him smile. "Do you remember the night you jumped into the lake?"

"Oh god." The one night I'd gotten too drunk in Maine—Talisker, again—I stripped down to my underwear and leapt into the cold water in front of everyone else at the residency.

"You looked like you were having fun."

"I was," I said. "I was having significantly too much fun."

His finger traced my hairline, tucking a piece behind me ear. "Is that what this is now, for you?" he asked. "Your one wild night?"

"No," I said, even though I wasn't sure.

"Then I want you to come out to the Berkshires."

I didn't answer, looking out the window at the triple across the street.

"I know I'm much older than you," he continued.

"The age isn't a thing," I said, a lie. The age was definitely a thing, although one that also excited me, an unusual stretch of distance.

"Spoken like a young person."

"I'm thirty. I use retinol," I said. "I'm not exactly *Lolita*." This was true, but also bullshit. I was no innocent, but I still stood at the beginning of my professional life while he lounged accomplished on the other side. I was *emerging*, a gerund, and he stood *established*, a state, all action in the past tense.

"No," he said, rolling toward me on the bed. He was almost ready again, thank god, and I started kissing his face, his neck, feeling the roughness where he needed to shave. "You're certainly not."

I stayed on my stomach, making him take me from behind with one hand braced against my back as the other worked the front of me. Still the careful space between us, like I was something costly cushioned by air. I arced my spine, wishing I could feel all of him against me. *More*, my body called, *harder*, until I was wrung out, finished.

I felt heavy afterward, my limbs weighted with irresistible day-sleep. I might have dozed for an hour, ten minutes. When I woke, the sun was still up. Confusing. My limbs splayed out across the bed, alone, and I could hear voices in the living room.

I got up, put my dress and underwear back on and tried to catch what they were saying. Maybe Annie would dazzle him. Annie often dazzled men. She didn't date them, but I'd notice her using this power in advantageous situations.

But when I opened the bedroom door, no one looked dazzled. He sat at the table by the bay window while Annie remained on the opposite side in the kitchen area, the cheap butcher-block island dividing them. She had both hands on the counter, her arms tense, like she might suddenly fling the furniture down and scatter our pots and pans.

"Hi," I said. "I see you're getting acquainted."

Annie didn't say anything. Unusual. "Yes," said the choreographer. "Annie is explaining that we're not technically in Boston."

"No," I said, joining Annie in the kitchen. "Somerville is a separate city. Do you want a drink?"

"Annie already got me one," said the choreographer, holding up a can of dry New England cider.

She shifted her body away from me as I walked to the fridge, holding herself with an odd, alert energy. "Everything alright?" I said to her, soft.

"Of course," she said. "I'm just—I'm going to go to my room."

"Okay," I said. She went into her bedroom and shut the door. The inner walls were not made well, and I could hear her moving things around, blasting Stevie Nicks.

All the while, the choreographer sat at my kitchen table, sipping, acting as if he belonged there.

"Rabbit," he said, "come here."

The words pulled on me like a leash. I walked over and sat on his lap. Under my short, loose dress, my bare thighs rubbed against the stiff fabric of his pants. He picked up his drink and pressed the cold metal against my forehead, my cheek, my neck.

"Oh, that's wonderful," I said, head tilted back.

"Good," he said. Then he put the can down and swam his hands up my skirt, brushing my skin.

His fingers worked around the elastic of my underwear, finding my center. I gasped and my pelvis jolted as he scooped his elbow under, working deeper, my muscles easing as the slow push of his hand unraveled me.

He yanked me forward so I fell against his neck. "Remember when I fucked you on my kitchen table?" he asked. I opened my mouth to speak but only made gutted animal sounds, his fingers taking the voice from me.

Then he pulled out, and I cried at the sudden emptiness. He picked up his can with the same hand that had just been inside me, taking a drink.

"I guess we can't do that here," he said.

Chapter Four

The Berkshires house dazzled so specifically it seemed built particularly for me. First, the approach, leaving the main highway for a two-lane road that hugged the edge of a foothill as the other side opened to views of the low valley. Here, in the mountains, the sunlight turned rarer, filtered and more golden.

Then the house itself, small and spare and seated back from the road near the rise of the ridge. The whole two-bedroom house centered around an old brick fireplace, the original hardwood floors buffed to a shine. Large, new windows opened everywhere to let in green and light, blurring the boundary between inside and out.

I looked through the books on his shelves. Art books, books on movement, and some of the more esoteric volumes that made up my own mother's milieu. Small tokens sat before the neat rows of spines: feathers and stones, the stubs of beeswax candles.

He'd built what I thought of as an altar by the front door, covering a small table with dark cloth. A vase of dry flowers sat next to an earthenware bowl of wishing stones, their dark bellies ringed with white. Next to them, a framed picture of his parents leaned against the wall. Age had bleached the color, obscuring the young people's expressions.

"Did your parents support your dancing?" I asked. He watched me move through his house from a careful distance, like I was a feral animal he'd just brought home.

"No," he said. "Not masculine enough."

Absurd, I thought. All that training had gifted him such a splendid male form.

"And yours?" he asked. "How do they feel about your writing?"

"They're supportive," I said. "I mean, sort of. They're writers, too. But mostly they're professors." My father tended to focus on "the sociology" of my fiction, while my mother, who claimed to be the only Asian American—language poet of her generation, railed against the novel as "the artform of the bourgeoisie." In these moments, she turned bug-eyed and wild, forgetting her academic appointment and house in Northwest Philly.

"That sounds helpful."

"Sometimes." I stopped, touching the spine of a Hélène Cixous dream book. "They have a lot of opinions."

On the wall in a dark, almost hidden corner hung a photograph of the choreographer caught in midleap. Even from the other side of the room, I could tell it was him from his form, his neck. His young skin radiated light, his body suspended with legs bent beneath him.

"You don't perform anymore," I said. A statement, knowledge I already had.

"No," he said.

"That must be—I imagine it's hard," I said.

"It is," he said. "But I was lucky. I went on for longer than most."

"Do you still . . ." I couldn't finish. The thought felt too overwhelming.

"Yes," he said. "I can still do a great deal. Just not that." He pointed to the photograph.

I wanted to see him dance, then. His body doing what it was intended for. "Will I ever see?"

He came close, his hands returning to the same spots on my torso as if he'd marked them. Kissing him still didn't feel like an entirely conscious act, just what happened given the right proximity. "Maybe," he said, "if you stick around."

He guided me to the back of the house and out the glass doors to the deck. A pond, which we could swim in, a wood-fired hot tub he'd built from a kit. The foothill rose above us, fenced off from the yard by the remains of an old stone wall. He described the different trails fanning out into the mountains. "We could take that one today," he said, pointing. "It's short. Leads to an old Shaker mill."

"I don't like Shakers," I said.

"What? What do you mean?"

"They freak me out."

"They're pacifists," he said. "Also, they don't exist anymore."

"Because they didn't have sex," I said. "So they could depopulate the planet." Mostly, though, I associated Shakers with childhood visits to the Philadelphia Museum of Art where the rooms of stark chairs preceded the horrifying Thomas Eakins medical paintings. My mother would hold me up to the canvas, forcing my gaze to the photo-real wound. "You have to look," she'd say. "He's a great Philadelphia artist."

"Maybe it wasn't the worst idea," the choreographer said, returning us to the Shakers. "And they channeled their eroticism in other ways."

"The furniture?"

"That, and they made wonderful dances."

He had his arm around me, my body sealed into his side. My skin began to wake up with the purpose of my visit.

"Do you like it?" he asked me.

I turned to hug him with both arms, standing front to front. "It's wonderful," I said. "Too much."

"I'm here most of the summer, so come whenever you like."

Our breathing didn't line up, pressed against each other. He looked crowned by the sun, haloed and golden. "Careful," I said, "or I'll be here every weekend."

"Rabbit," he said, his mouth tipping down to mine, "I believe that's the idea."

I SPENT THE summer so drunk with sex that all my driving shouldn't have been allowed, back and forth between Boston and the Berkshires, cutting through long mountain detours to avoid traffic on the Mass Pike. I was at his house, or I was off to his house, or I imagined myself there, wandering the administrative offices of the Economics Department dazed by a full body-craving.

My life split in two. During the week: the office, the city, meeting friends for drinks or cooking dinner at home with Annie. Reading and talking and waking up in the morning to scribble in a notebook.

But on the weekends I let go; I disappeared, my brain scattering as I abandoned the structures of my life. My body took the lead, beaming and bright like a fire beacon.

Someone needed to do something. Someone needed to put me out.

ONE WEDNESDAY, ANNIE texted saying, to meet her at the German bar down the hill after work. We lived at the bar when we didn't live in our apartment. "We need you to stay this weekend," she told me once we'd settled in.

I sniffed my free drink. Sweet, like licorice. The bartender slipped us something new each night; she'd become a friend, we were there so often. "Who's we, and why?"

"Esme is in crisis." Esme was our other friend from college. After grad school, I left Amherst to return to Esme and Annie, to Boston and their familiar gravity.

"The twenty-five-year-old?" For the last two months, Esme had been seeing a younger woman, an Allston quasi-punk who may or may not have worked in IT.

"Ghosted," Annie said.

"Fuck."

"Right," Annie said. "We need you there. For triage."

"Of course," I said.

"So you'll tell him? That you're staying?"

I paused, putting down the shot glass. Annie didn't sound insistent, just nervous. "Sure," I said. "Like I said, I'll be there."

"Okay." She picked up her identical drink. "Cheers, then. To love."

We tinked our glasses, facing each other on our stools. I thought I saw an unfamiliar wariness. But once the liquor was down, Annie coughed and smiled and we laughed together for no reason.

I called Esme that night. The twenty-five-year-old had stopped calling or texting while still posting pictures of herself eating hot sauce or jumping into the Mystic River. "What did I do?" Esme said over the phone. "What did I do wrong?"

I shushed her. "You didn't do anything," I said. "It's going to be okay."

That weekend, we filled our bike panniers with grocery store salami and soft cheeses, crackers and grapes and prerolled spliffs, then biked over to the Esplanade to ply Esme with consumable comfort. She wouldn't touch any of it, mooning away at the gorgeous day.

"She's an asshole," Annie said.

"I just thought she would have had more respect," Esme said, staring straight through flocks of fuzzy baby geese. They bobbed on the dark water like fluffy tennis balls.

"Isn't she twenty-five?" I said.

"Twenty-four."

"There you go," I said. "Remember when we were twenty-four?" I had vivid alcohol-soaked memories of Esme hooking up with a woman in the bathroom of a Dunkin' Donuts after a dance party at the Middle East.

"In some ways I think I was wiser then," Esme said.

I touched her back, petted her wild red hair.

"Do you think the age difference was too much?" Esme asked.

"No," I said, turning hot. "Not really. But a lot happens in the twenties. Like your brain finishes developing."

Annie looked at me with such intensity that the surface of my skin burned.

"Maybe I freaked her out," Esme said.

"No," I said. "You didn't do anything wrong."

"Yeah, fuck her," Annie said.

Esme shook her head. "That's exactly what I can't do."

Eventually, Esme moved on to the next batch of comforting friends, leaving Annie and I with the feast. I cracked a cider can and laid back on the warm wood of the dock, all worn out from compassion.

"Ugh, poor Ez," I said, watching a windsurfer flop into the water. "We're too old for ghosting."

"I know," Annie said, lighting a spliff. "That girl's a jerk. I hope Ez snaps out of it soon."

She handed the spliff to me, squinting from the sun. "So you really don't think anything crucial happens to the brain in the thirties?"

I hugged my knees, hunchbacked at the end of the dock. "Or the forties," I said, taking a puff.

"Damn," Annie said. She pinched the spliff away from my fingers. "I thought only girls with daddy issues dated old men. But your father's a nice guy."

"Oh, shut up," I said, throwing a grape, but I smiled. "And I'm not a girl, I'm a woman."

Annie caught the grape and popped it in her mouth. "You know he's going to die way before you?" she said, tucking the fruit into her cheek.

I took the spliff back. She'd smeared the end with her tinted lip balm, but I smoked from it anyway. "I don't think we're really at the 'When are we going to die?' stage yet."

Annie picked up a salami slice, ripping into it with her front teeth. "This is new for you," she said, looking at me.

"What? The older guy thing?" I said.

She nodded. "And the chasing."

I sat up now. "I'm not chasing," I said.

"You're out there every weekend."

"It's nice out there. It's nature."

"You've lived in Western Mass before," said Annie. "I don't think you're driving out just to take in the scenery."

In a different mood, I would have made a joke. *Depends on the kind of scenery.* But I didn't. I remembered Annie's hesitancy at the bar, the birth of some new doubt.

My phone buzzed. The choreographer. *Can you talk tonight?*

"That him?" she said, looking at the phone.

"It is."

She smirked, some knowledge about me confirmed.

"What does he want?" she asked.

"Nothing," I said. "Just to talk."

Annie reached over, taking the spliff from me and flicking off the ash I'd let build up. "What do you like about him?"

I didn't understand. "You mean, like, qualities?"

"Yeah," Annie said. "Like, is he funny? Or smart? Why him?"

I remembered the lightning bolt down my lower back as we sat together at the bar. My sudden certainty.

"Or is it just because of the sex?" Annie said. The way she asked, I could tell she already had decided it wasn't.

"I guess it isn't," I said. "But, I don't know. I haven't really thought about it yet."

Another text message. *I miss you.* I picked up the phone, feeling its density and heft.

"I—he's very interested. In me. I think," I said. My words seemed dull against the weight of his attention, heavy even through the phone.

"He better," Annie said. "Or he's an idiot."

I took another puff from the spliff and handed it off before sending back a quick text. *out now will txt when home.*

"But what's wrong with Boston?" Annie said. "Why can't he come here?"

I saw Annie's face at the kitchen counter, the way she'd braced herself for attack. "Do you want him to come here?"

"Of course," Annie said. "If he's going to be in your life, then I should know him. He should get to know all of us."

In my life. But was that where I wanted him? I couldn't imagine him in Somerville, eating takeout Nepalese, smoking weed. I couldn't see him standing at the German bar under Annie's interrogation. And, more surprising, I didn't want to, for once. I wanted him there, on the outside.

Annie handed back the spliff. "Okay," I said, squeezing it between my fingers. "We'll see."

I finished smoking, letting the weed ease me so I could take in the city's peak beauty. Sunlight shone off the river, the state capitol dome, while pleasure boats chugged toward the harbor. Buzzed from the spliff, I found the city's abundant pleasantness overwhelming.

In such states of open comfort, I sometimes fell into the delusion that Annie and I built all the beauty in our lives through the sheer force of our proximity. Her presence became a shelter, a guide, a shared perspective buoyed by a certainty neither one of us could carry alone. Together, the world sharpened into focus, the murky parts of my life moving into light.

Even the dullness of our first post-college jobs became an adventure with Annie. She'd visit me at the bookstore I worked at in Harvard Square, sneaking me away from behind the cash register to find the spot on the shelves where our books would one day sit. She'd point out authors I'd never heard of and tell me what to buy. And then, when the bookstore closed, I'd walk down the street to the bar where she worked, accepting free gin and tonics until it was time for the two of us to stumble home. The early-morning streets lost their danger as long as we were together.

Many different versions of us stood between the girls we had been and the women we were now, our identities layered like ancient rock. A harder Annie had emerged, one with goals and a vision board and a clear idea of the points she wanted to put on her CV. And I'd become a headier person, one made of references and theories. But I wanted to believe some core of us still remained. Even now, sitting by the water, I looked at Annie's white sneakers hanging off the dock and saw her at eighteen. I felt returned, the same, my whole life stretching behind me.

The light turned long and saturated, the fated golden hour. I stretched out on my back, my fingers resting on the knit of my ribs. "I don't think I can get up," I said. "I think I have to live here now."

She laughed, standing up. Grabbing my ankle, she tugged me along the splintery wood, her hands a warm brace on my leg. "Up you go," she said, "or you'll be eaten by geese."

"No, I won't," I said, smiling at her. "You'll fend them off."

She dropped the ankle and pulled me up by my wrist. "I'll try," she promised, her other hand steadying me. "But they'll defeat me."

We biked home as the sun began to set, crossing the water below drastic streaks of pink and blue. Annie rode ahead of me, sometimes pulling so far away I could only spot her by the blonde hair flying behind her like a flag. Tall, athletic, she turned easily to pure motion, her desires bolstered by an effervescent sense of permissiveness. If I pulled close, I sometimes felt her power rippling off, pulling me along in the wake of her belief.

By the time we got home, I was sweaty, and the hour was late. "Do you want to watch something?" Annie asked as we finished putting the food in the fridge.

"Maybe in a bit," I said. I held up my phone.

"Ah," Annie said, looking away.

Alone in my room, the door closed, I called the choreographer.

"Hello, Rabbit," he said. My skin prickled, the hair raising along my neck. "Did you have a good time?"

"I did," I said, stretching out on top of my bedspread. I still felt a little stoned, the weed cooling me. "We biked down to the river. Had a picnic."

"Who was there?"

"Just Annie and our friend Esme," I said. "Esme is in heartbreak."

"Tragedy," the choreographer said.

I closed my eyes. Everyone else I knew used video chat, but I liked this, just hearing his voice, imagining him pacing around his house in the middle of the mountains.

"What did you do today?" I asked.

"Read. Missed you. Saw some friends."

My skin buzzed against the fabric. Still stoned. "You missed me, hm?" I repeated.

"I did," he said. "Very much."

I felt the question in my throat, on my tongue. *Come here. Meet my people.* But I didn't let it out, swallowing it back.

"I'll be there next weekend," I said.

I imagined him in his kitchen, at his altar, looking out at his things.

"Good."

THE WEATHER TURNED vividly hot even in the mountains. I took a dip alone in the pond, floating on my back as the water slipped over my bare skin. He'd fitted the pond with a silent filtration system, lining its borders with purifying plants to keep the water clean. Against the bright background of the sky, I picked out a dark shadow, some taloned bird of prey.

Where was he? Flipping upright, I scanned the yard and found the choreographer by the tree line, staring into the forest through a pair of miniature binoculars.

"What are you doing?" I asked, paddling closer.

"I think I hear a northern mockingbird."

"That's the most old-man thing I've ever seen you do," I told him.

"Really? I heard it's the new millennial craze."

I sucked in a breath, dunking myself under to cool my face and listen to the strange sounds of the water. Wrinkly, done, I swam to the dock and pushed myself out.

He dropped the binoculars and turned away from the forest, watching my bare body as I crossed to the Adirondack chairs. Small blades of grass stuck to my wet feet, and I squeezed my hair dry with my towel before wrapping the fabric tight around myself.

Dropping back into the chair, I eased into the warm wood, closing my eyes and listening to him approach.

"A couple of friends just got into Lenox," he said, taking the seat next to me.

"Mm." So he probably wanted to drive over to see them. I got ready to tell him I didn't mind spending the evening alone.

"They want to come over for dinner. Is that okay?"

I propped myself up, eyes open. "They want to eat here?" I repeated. "How are you going to explain me?"

"I was planning to just say you're my partner," he said. "That's the term now, right?"

I settled back into the chair, lower and deeper than before. "I'm your partner, huh?" The word brought a new structure, a fresh box encasing me.

"How do you explain me to your friends. To Annie?"

I didn't. I stayed quiet.

"Are you nervous?"

"No," I said. "Why would I be nervous?"

I got up, went back into the house to shower. He followed. "So they're not really friends," he continued. "They're donors."

I stopped walking and turned to face him. My bare, wet feet squeaked on the wood. "Ah."

"I'd try to push the dinner to the week, but . . ." His empty hands twisted in the air, miming beggary.

"It's okay," I said.

"They're going to be a lot."

"I deal with econ professors all day," I said. "I understand *a lot*."

I got in the shower to wash off the essence of pond, then dug around in my bag for something that didn't say "younger sex friend." I picked tan linen pants, a plain black blouse, some jade earrings that had belonged to my mother. Then minimal makeup and twisting my dark hair into a braid.

As I helped the choreographer set the table, I had the eerie feeling that I was putting out cloth placemats at my parents' house. The good silver, fine napkins, brass holders for the candles. He uncorked the reds, letting them breathe, then took care to properly chill the whites.

"You are nervous," he said as I checked my reflection in one of the decorative hall mirrors.

"I am." I turned to him. "I wasn't expecting to play hostess in your life tonight."

He held me close, kissed my forehead. "You'll be wonderful."

Their names were actually Franny and Dodge. They came in fresh and smelling of peonies, Franny dressed in what I thought of as a "summer cardigan." They hugged me with only their hands. The choreographer's face turned tight as he spoke to them, showing too many teeth. They must have given a lot of money.

We had pasta with white beans and grilled vegetables, Parmesan cheese served on the side. I watched Franny use her knife to push a piece of asparagus up the tines of her fork.

"So, dear," Franny said to me. "What do you do?"

"I work at Harvard," I said.

"You teach?"

"No," I said. "I'm an administrative coordinator. I work in the Econ Department."

"That must be very interesting," said Dodge. His head was fully bald with a spot on its top that needed a medical opinion.

"It's mostly office work."

"She's also a writer," said the choreographer. "She's very disciplined. She gets up at five every day to work."

"Five A.M., goodness," said Franny. "I could never wake up that early."

"It's what I've got," I said. "I wouldn't say it's when I do my best work."

"What do you write about?" asked Dodge.

Don't say capitalism. "Many things."

The quiet lasted too long. My parents always put Yo-Yo Ma on in the background for just this reason.

"Franny also went to Wellesley," the choreographer said to me.

Franny turned to me as if she'd just discovered some unexpected treasure, pure delight. "You're a Wellesley woman?"

"I am."

"Gosh, I made such wonderful memories there. I lived in Beebe Hall."

I fingered my first girlfriend in Beebe Hall. "I have such wonderful memories, too," I said.

I tried to think of the oldest person I knew at Wellesley. "Did you know Ms. Pierce, the Romance Languages librarian?"

"Yes!" said Franny. "She's still there? She completely saved my thesis paper."

"Mine, too," I said. I worked my face into a smile, a thin line of friendliness.

They'd brought apple pie with butter in the crust, so the choreographer just put a piece on his plate and picked around, pretending to eat.

"Will you be at his talk on Tuesday?" Dodge asked me.

"I wish, but I can't," I said. The choreographer spent his weekdays working at the big summer-long dance festival nearby. Teaching, giving talks, a premiere of new work scheduled for the end of the summer. "I have to go back to work."

"Maybe you could use some vacation days," the choreographer said to me. I shook my head.

"I'm still earning time back after Maine."

"You've already been to Maine this summer?" said Franny. I looked at the choreographer. I needed a break.

"Maine is where we met," he said. "At a residency."

"Is that one of those programs where they feed you?" Franny said. "They sound so wonderful. I've thought about doing one sometime."

He didn't have to do much with his face. A slight crinkle above his right eyebrow, looking at me from a different angle. I felt the mocking clear, and my own mocking met his in return. Who knew we could talk like this, without betraying ourselves, without ever saying a word?

At the end of the evening, we had to guide and nudge them out the door, letting them finally slosh their way down the drive.

He rubbed my shoulders, kissing my neck. "You were wonderful," he said. "Do you want me to start a fire under the hot tub?"

The heat let up with the setting sun, the mountain air turning cool. The choreographer got out of the water before me to do some work, and I stayed alone under the great carpet of Western Massachusetts stars. Sinking up to my shoulders, I listened to the distant hoots of an owl, the hum of summer insects lighting up the forest. Franny and Dodge paid for all of this, at least in part, and I paid them back with smiling, with cultured entertainment. *Money and power and sex and devotion.* Alone in the darkness, I played with the four words like marbles.

The fire below the wooden tub died, leaving the water to cool rapidly. I got out and poured a pitcher down the cast-iron spout to dampen the embers before tugging the cover back in place. Tightening my yellow robe around me, I finger-combed my wet hair and slipped inside.

The choreographer sat on the couch, glasses on, his face illuminated by the glow of his laptop. I found my book and made a cup of chamomile tea. Carrying my mug and *Good Morning, Midnight*, I settled down next to him.

"What do you think of her?" he asked, tilting his computer toward me. Jackie appeared in a sheer yellow skirt and bikini top, draped over the shoulder of a male dancer. Her pretty, pointed face looked arrested, surprised, her limbs electric and tense.

"She seems great," I said, blowing on my tea. Her hips stuck through the skirt. *Iliac crests.* "Have you slept with her?" I asked.

"No," he said. He turned to me. "I'd never sleep with a dancer I paid."

I dangled my tea bag. "But you've slept with other dancers."

"Haven't you slept with other writers?"

"Only unfortunately." The tea seemed strong enough. I pulled the bag out and squeezed.

He looked back at the screen. "She's working with TJ and Zac on the trio for the festival," he said. "She's very talented, very strong. But I need her to forget her strength for the piece. She needs to be more open in her body."

"What does that mean?" I asked.

He brought his fingers to the screen, pinching across her shoulders.

"She always holds her scapula tight, protecting the heart area. She's too much of a performer, can't let go into the movement. The pretending never becomes real."

His hand left the keyboard, his thumb stroking my inner elbow. "I wish I could get them to be more like you."

"What? Like a hobbity gremlin?" I said.

"That's how you think of yourself?"

"That's how I think of all writers," I said, sipping. "You shouldn't want them to be like me. I'm not self-conscious in my body because I'm barely aware I have one."

"You seem pretty aware to me."

I turned to kiss his ear. "I'm only like that with you."

The gesture juddered through him, a tightening followed by release. "Is something wrong?" I asked.

He pressed the back of his hand against mine. "No," he said. "Not at all."

I looked back at his laptop. Jackie in a different pose, being lifted into the air by her ankle. "Why did you—what made you stop performing?" I asked. I knew why, of course. But I wanted to hear specifics.

He scrolled to the next image. A male dancer, I think Zac, in midleap. "I made this part for myself, once," he said, pointing at the screen. "But then—bad back. Bad knees, sprained ankles. I herniated a disc and knew it was time to step aside and let the young shine."

He kept his voice light, but I heard an unfamiliar pain, a new ache and depth that hooked under my ribs and tugged. I wanted to press my mouth to what he'd named, his shattered parts. "Can you put the computer away?" I asked.

I slid into his lap, kissing him with an open mouth, his lips parted but restrained.

"You want this even though I'm broken?" he said, pushing open my robe.

"Yes," I said. "Please."

My fingers wove into his hair and clutched the back of his skull as his hand slipped between my legs. His touch caught and grounded me, tethering me to my flesh.

He burrowed his face into my sternum, his breath hot. Against my skin, he said, "You should move to New York."

I went rigid, a caught animal. "What?" I leaned away and took my hands off him. Still perched on his knees, I pulled the robe closed. "No way."

I thought he'd wake up, agree. But he said, "Why not?"

"I'd have to upend my whole life," I said. "I'd have to find a new place to live."

"You could stay with me for a while." He held the sides of my waist.

"Ha, yeah, right," I said. "I could never afford your place."

He looked up into my face. "You wouldn't have to pay."

Now the blood went the way of my muscles, everything solid, frozen. "I couldn't do that," I said softly.

"Why not?"

"My lease." My lungs filled, the pressure pushing into my throat, behind my eyes.

"Break it."

"My job."

"You hate it," he said. "You wouldn't have to work. You could write."

"No," I said, leaning back. I didn't know what frightened me more, the speed or size of his offer.

The force of my refusal entered him, pushing him back. He took a breath, gripping around my ribs as he looked away from me.

"Fine," he said. He turned his attention back to my body, his mouth at my collarbone as his fingers reached for the edge of my robe. "It was just an idea."

We moved forward into sex, but even in the middle of pleasure I still remained confused. Until that afternoon, I hadn't even known I was his *partner*. Such a heavy, public word.

In the morning, I woke late, catching up on all the sleep I had missed during the week, thanks to the early-morning writing sessions. Still under the covers, I watched him cross the open doorway, lovely in his sleeping clothes, a T-shirt and plain gray cotton pants. *He really likes me,* I thought, but I didn't feel what I expected, the initial giddy thrill. Instead, there was fright, and I knew then that I stood on the edge of an unfamiliar precipice.

We drove up to MASS MoCA, wandering through the huge industrial galleries and staring at suspended coils molded by Louise Bourgeois. There we were, the two of us, reflected in the shine and gleam of metal.

We stopped in front of a Robert Rauschenberg. The sculpture had been built from old wood and rusted saws, joints bare and paint flaking. "Do you remember when that conceptual sound artist spilled wine all over Julie's new lake paintings?" I asked.

He laughed, like I knew he would, then choked it down with his fist to his mouth. "I shouldn't laugh," he said. "That was awful. Poor Julie."

"But it was funny," I said.

"I'm surprised you remember. You jumped in the lake that night."

"Her howls penetrated even my drunkenness."

He wrapped his arm around my shoulder, pulling my body into his. I let my head drift against his chest, testing the posture.

"What is this to you?" I asked, still looking at the sculpture.

"You mean us?" he said. I shifted my head slightly to look up at him. "Not a summer fling."

"So you want more?" I said. I tried to keep the flirt out of my voice. My face stayed plain and serious.

He reached across with his other hand, touching my jaw, my cheek. "Oh, yes," he said.

On my own, I went into a temporary exhibit, a big dark room with a bright window at the end. Glass separated the viewer from a chamber of ice. Ice on the walls, on the ceilings, all in defiance of the hot summer day. A square hole had been cut into the middle of the floor, just big enough for a single person to fit through. At random times, the wall placard warned, you might see the artist emerge.

I stayed in the dark room longer than anyone else. I stepped close to the glass, willing the cold through. If I stayed, maybe I could find my way into the room. Then I'd drop down, disappear. I'd cool myself. I'd find a way to stay.

Chapter Five

Time folded itself differently when we were in the mountains, the creases looser and more fluid as if the weekends could take up more hours than all the other days of the week. At the end of July, I woke in his bed, dazed. How did I get here, at the edge of August, the month of Sunday-feeling?

Jackie came to the Berkshires with the rest of the trio in preparation for the performance. They stayed at the festival's accommodations across the valley, but the choreographer invited them over for dinner a week before. He made a big salad, bowls of quinoa and farro, grilled tofu and eggplant. I stared at all the food as I put it out, wishing I'd remembered to sneak in a pizza.

The dancers came together in TJ's Honda Civic. The boys—they were young enough to be boys—wore collared shirts, pants. Jackie had on a short red dress with big chunks bitten out of the midriff. They held themselves stiff, nervous about showing up at their boss's for dinner.

I greeted them at the door in my olive-green romper, playing house.

"This is so lovely," said TJ, looking up at the rising foothills.

"Isn't it?" I said, pretending I was not such a newcomer as well.

I let them into the house and watched as they studied the shelves, the altar, my own feeling reflected in their expressions. So awed by the handsome existence, one that I still felt like a pretender in.

"Can I get you anything?" I asked. My voice sounded light and strange. I remembered a party my parents had thrown when I was a child. I'd appointed myself the coat taker, a pint of a person standing by the door with a stack of cloth on top of me. I felt like that again, playing grown-up, looking for a task. "Snacks? A drink? He's out back grilling."

"What do you have?" asked TJ.

"Almost everything," I said.

"What are you drinking?" asked Zac.

"A gin and tonic."

"That sounds good," Zac said. "Like, easy."

I mixed the drinks in the kitchen. The knowledge that the choreographer was out in the backyard kept the dancers inside with me, hovering as I measured ice and squeezed limes.

I felt comfortably older than TJ and Zac. Their skin looked so perfect it was almost translucent, their bodies full of bounding energy. But Jackie, I couldn't tell. She wore full makeup, the foundation giving her face an artificial luster so I couldn't judge its wear and age. I had the urge to smear the surface with a washcloth, exposing the real skin underneath.

"I like your earrings," said Jackie. I had on the jade ones again.

"Thank you," I said. "Nice dress."

Snacks. I'd forgotten the snacks. "There's nuts and stuff. Here," I said, grabbing a bowl from the other end of the counter and pushing it in front of them. "Do you have any dietary restrictions?"

"Vegan," said TJ.

"No meat," said Zac. "And, like, gluten."

"I'm keto," Jackie said.

I swallowed, panicked. "Are nuts okay, then?"

"Yeah, totally fine." They all agreed, nodding, and took a few cashews in order to please me.

The choreographer appeared, slipping through the back door. The dancers tightened, their posture straightening. "Darling, you didn't tell me the guests had arrived," he said, hugging me with one arm and kissing my forehead. He touched me often, but in front of others the gestures felt showy, as if he were planting little flags.

"I was getting them drinks," I said, my voice slipping into the role of partner and good hostess.

The dancers picked up the glasses in front of them, remembering their props.

"One for you, too," I said, handing over a glass. I drank a little more from mine, took some nuts to steady myself or it would be another night of jumping into water.

"Should we show them around?" the choreographer said.

He took them on a modified version of the tour he'd given me. The pond, the trail to the Shaker mill, the roses now in full bloom. I followed along, mute, as if I were just another feature of the house.

"Fresh drinks," he said, noticing their empty glasses.

The alcohol and the gorgeousness of the mountains began to put the dancers at ease. My presence, I realized, helped as well. I wasn't as old as the choreographer, maybe not properly an adult. As we got closer to dinner, the boys began to flirt and tease me even as they wrapped their limbs around each other, Zac's mouth plucking grapes from TJ's fingertips.

"Where did you get your romper?" Jackie asked, looking at the hem of my shorts.

"I don't know," I said. I heated, staring at my own bare thigh. "I think a thrift store."

"You have such pretty feet," said Zac, looking at my unabused toes. The dancers all wore closed-toed shoes, hiding battered and bleeding appendages.

How old were Zac and TJ? Twenty-one, twenty-two? Boys, I called them, but I was so much closer in age to them than to the choreographer.

By the time we reached the meal, the dancers had fully relaxed, so open in their physicality that the air around us turned combustible. My attention kept turning to Jackie. The turn of her wrists, hair flicking from side to side. I'd never been so close to a woman fully present in her body. No superfluous gestures, each movement under her control.

"Is that, like, a blue jay?" asked Zac, squinting at a bird in the bush.

"Brown-headed cowbird," corrected the choreographer.

"Wait, let me add it to my bird-watching app," said TJ, taking out his phone. The choreographer glanced at me, and I turned to keep away the gratification of a smile.

"Do you get bored out here?" Zac asked. "Like, is there a town?"

"There are many towns. Lenox, Great Barrington," the choreographer said. "But no." And his hand found my thigh under the table, the pressure light and warm. "We don't get bored."

After dinner, I helped the choreographer clean up in the kitchen while the dancers stayed out back.

"You don't have to do this," he told me as I dried one of the serving platters.

"It's fine," I said. The tasks gave me something specific to do, chores to push away my discomfort.

"Really, stop," he said, squeezing my shoulder and kissing the top of my head. "Go keep them entertained. They'll be more relaxed around you."

I looked out the window at Jackie standing on the dock. I dried my hands on the dishcloth. "Okay."

I fixed two gin and tonics, sipping mine as I crossed the lawn.

"Brought you a fresh drink," I said, holding out the glass.

"Thanks." She smiled as she took it, the air around her thickened with perfume. *Tuberose*, I thought. What would Annie think of her? Annie sometimes struggled to relate to other femmes. "You came to our rehearsal once, right? I remember you."

"Good memory," I said, stepping closer. She held herself like the choreographer. Upright, her limbs both strong and supple.

"Were you a dancer, too?"

"No." I drank. I'd been drinking, and now I stood too close to her on the wide, spacious dock. "My thing was soccer. Kicking other little girls' shins."

"You don't really seem like that," she said. "You seem nice."

"Maybe when I'm not on the field."

The boys were rolling in the grass, showing off their leaps. She looked at them, then at me. I made her nervous, a fact that thrilled me.

"This is so lovely," she said, pointing with her toe at the water. "Can you swim in it?"

I nodded. "We can swim now if you'd like."

She returned her bare foot to the dock, shaking her head. "I don't have my suit."

"You don't need one," I said. I raised my glass to the trees. "No neighbors."

"That's nice." Another *nice*. I thought at first she looked uncomfortable because I was being lecherous, but then she glanced back at the patio, the house, and I realized she was thinking about me and the choreographer out here, that I was the woman fucking her boss.

Zac joined us on the dock, swinging his arms around our necks. "Where does that go?" he said, looking at the trailhead.

"Up the ridge, so you can look out at the valley," I said. "Then it meets up with the Appalachian Trail."

"Can we go?" He released us, running back to TJ. "TJ, you want to go for a hike?"

"No," the choreographer said, stepping through the back door. "None of you have on the right shoes."

"These are orthopedic," said TJ, pointing at his feet.

"And you've been drinking." He walked up to the dock, grabbed my glass from my hand, and took a long pull. "The last thing I need is for one of you to break an ankle."

"I'm perfectly sober," TJ insisted. "I'm designated-driving."

The choreographer handed my drink back, and in just that gesture, the way he looked at me, I saw, somehow, that he knew.

"The trail is smooth and short," I said. "We can be up and back before sundown."

I felt him study me, inspecting. I kept my face still, refusing to give anything away.

"Whatever you want, darling," he said.

He got out little spray bottles of all-natural tick repellant and made everyone put some on. "I don't want anyone getting Lyme disease. Particularly you." He caught me in an arm, wrapping me close and kissing me on the mouth in front of the boys and Jackie. I flushed and pushed him away. He definitely knew.

I sprayed some of the repellant on my neck, my arms, turning into a bomb of citronella and rosemary. "It doesn't really work," I told Jackie, handing her the bottle, "but we can do a tick check afterward."

The choreographer led, and I brought up the rear behind Zac, whose long legs took in the trail faster than I could keep up. "This is such a pretty place to spend the summer," he said.

"I'm only here on the weekends," I said. "I live in Boston."

"Oh. You don't live in New York?

"No." I knew what Zac was thinking. Not in New York. Not with the choreographer.

"Is Boston . . . nice?"

"It can be," I huffed.

We got to the ridge, the view of the valley. The choreographer pointed to a spot on the opposite side. "That's where the festival stage is," he told the dancers. "That's where you'll perform next weekend."

The dancers went quiet, staring with their naked eyes at the hump of land and trees. They seemed to stretch and drift, tuned in through the fine instrument of their bodies. Finally, I understood. The performance would be a big deal.

We made it back to the house before the sun set, and the dancers started their thank-yous, their goodbyes, off to a party on the festival grounds.

Jackie stopped me, her hand on my bare arm. "You said you would do a tick check."

"Sure." I made her turn around, lifting her hair so I could see where the growth met her pale skin. Her dress was backless, her skin peppered with one or two full, 3D moles. I ran my fingertip along the hairline, behind the whorls of her delicate ears. She had a light freckle on the back of the left one. I wondered if she knew about it.

Lingering, I stopped myself from touching the knobs of her cervical spine. "All clear." I let go of her hair, the sheet of it dropping against her bare shoulder blades.

"Thanks," she said, running down to the car. "See you next weekend."

I waved, watching the car back up. And then the choreographer stepped behind me, lifting my hair, his finger tracing my ears in an exact imitation. At the last moment, he pressed his mouth against the back of my neck. My skin tingled, but I couldn't tell if it was with thrill or warning.

"You have one, darling," he said, letting my hair fall. "Let me go get the tweezers."

WE BUILT A fire that night, sitting on the Adirondack chairs and listening to the logs crackle and burst.

"Are you sorry you didn't go with them?" he said, and I knew he meant the dancers.

"No," I said, bringing up my feet and tucking in my knees. "I'm too old for whatever they're doing."

"But are you too young for this?" He held out his hand. I took it, wrapping my fingers around his palm.

"No," I said. "I don't think so."

He hummed, a neutral sound.

For a moment, he looked out into the woods, quiet. "You like Jackie," he said.

"She's nice."

"You know that's not what I mean."

I inhaled deeply and stretched my feet back out, letting them toast in the fire's heat. "Was it obvious?"

"To me it was."

I couldn't read his voice. He could control it, clean it when he wanted to.

"Are you jealous?"

"A little," he admitted. "But mostly I'm curious."

He'd put too many logs on the fire. I started to sweat. "Why?"

"I want to know what you like," he said, "so I can give it to you."

"You can't give me Jackie."

"Rabbit." The name felt like a choke around my neck. "You know what I mean."

The choke spread across my body, a full-skin squeeze that shifted into an exterior pulse.

I chose my words, picking them out and placing them with care.

"My last girlfriend didn't like that I spaced out after I came," I said. "She thought I'd go blank, or like, dissociate. She kept on looking for trauma or something."

"And your last boyfriend?"

"He didn't make me come at all."

He laughed, and I felt the pulse respond, growing like disturbed bioluminescence.

I could see the dock by the almost-full moon, filled in by the light spilling from the house. I heard the water slap against the wood. "I'm hot," I said. "I'm going to take a dip."

I walked toward the pond, pulling off the romper, my underwear, losing each piece in the dark grass. The choreographer watched, the silver moonlight sliding down my back.

I got to the edge. I was wrong. I was freezing. But still I stepped off, straight down. Splash, then sink, nothing left but plunge.

Chapter Six

On Sunday evening, I returned to Somerville, feeling tired and odd as I stepped into the apartment. My life, waiting to fold me back in.

Annie's door stood open, but her room was dark. Unsettled, I wandered around the empty rooms, popping a seltzer and looking for snacks. Finally, I landed on the couch, reading until I heard her key in the lock.

"Hey," she said, smiling. "You're back."

I sat up so I could look at her over the back of the couch. "Had to come back sometime," I said. She wore a black romper, almost the same cut as my green one. Had we bought them together? I couldn't remember.

"I thought you wouldn't be back until late." She tugged off her sandals. Her legs were long and muscular, a product of all the biking.

"You expecting someone? You want me to skedaddle?" I asked, leaning my chin on the plush back of the sofa.

She shook her head, laughing. "No. I'm happy to see you."

What would my summer have looked like without the choreographer? I hadn't been out to Cape Cod with Annie even once. Usually, we spent the hot months hiding at her parents' beach house, an escape from the humidity. "Good," I said. "How was your night? Where are you coming from?"

"SoWa," she said. "It was fun. There was a reading at this group art gallery, the one Janice is part of." She hung her purse on one of the hooks we'd drilled into the walls in defiance of our lease. I loved her purse, the belly of the bag sculpted like tulip petals or fat licks of flame. An heirloom, something her mother had bought when she was our age on a tour of Paris. In college, Annie had worn the purse to class when all the rest of us still slouched around with our monogrammed L.L.Bean backpacks. I'd noticed her because of that bag. *Who is this girl?* I'd thought, or maybe, *Who is this woman?*, because the leather petals signaled someone with adult attentions and tastes.

"Who's Janice?" I asked, watching Annie unhook her hoop earrings and drop them on the mail table. I'd warned her to stop doing that. They always got swept up and disappeared with the junk.

"I set you up with Janice. Remember?"

Janice. "That poet you work with?"

Annie clucked her tongue. "That's *Jess.* I also set you up with her."

Damn. "You set me up with a lot of people," I said.

"Apparently." She came over and rubbed my hair, the way she might touch a pet. "And none of them take."

She yawned and went into her room, leaving the door open. I heard the thud of her dresser drawer, the rustle of fabric as she changed. The sounds of Annie undoing herself, a routine I'd listened to each day. Now she would go wash her face free of makeup, start her skin routine. She'd pull her hair into a bun and stick a retainer in her mouth.

I got up from the couch and slipped through her open door. I wanted more of her familiarity. Her clean, neat room, a curated bohemian lair ready to tip into real affluence. Books I'd borrowed, spare paintings she'd taken from her parents' collection, dried flowers to adorn her dresser and an antique egg cup to hold her gold rings. A decade-old amazement still settled over me as I walked into her space, a buzzing attraction to her knowledge and elegance and taste.

In bed, Annie sat propped up on her pillows, phone in hand.

"Can I get in?" I asked.

"Of course."

I pulled back the corner of Annie's thin floral blanket and climbed underneath. Her linens smelled specific, the comfort of name-brand detergent.

Flat on my back, I looked up at the view that greeted Annie every day. A neat, multicolored row of same-sized books dominated the top shelf: all *The Best American Short Stories* since 1999, the year Annie announced to her family that she wanted to be a writer. Her parents met the declaration by buying her the new volume every year. The paperbacks signaled Annie's sureness, her hope and clarity. She carted them through our dorm rooms, our shitty apartments, and now they crowned the cusp of our real adult lives. Less books than talismans, proof of seriousness and effort.

"Anything good in there?" I asked, looking at her phone.

"No." She slammed it facedown on the bedcovers. "Just Twitter."

"You need to delete the app."

"I know. But work." She covered her face for a moment, breathing into her hands. "Ugh, whatever. How was your weekend?"

I rolled away from the bookshelf, curled on my side facing her. "People came over to his house. For dinner. His dancers." I thought about naming Jackie.

"Mm. And they know about you?" she said.

"Of course. Why wouldn't they?"

"I mean, you never talk about him," Annie said. "About what you are."

"You don't ask."

"I'm respecting your privacy."

"What privacy?" I said. In college, Annie used to follow me into the bathroom at parties, drunkenly crying, "I'm lonely."

Annie slid down from the pillows so our heads were even, looking at me. "You don't exactly seem excited to talk about it," she said.

I reached around to touch the back of my neck, the ridge of bone where I still felt his mouth.

"You guys . . . you don't seem like a summer thing," Annie said.

I felt his fingers on my jaw, pulling my face up. "No. I don't think so," I said.

"But he lives in New York."

"I know."

"And he's . . ." But she stopped, looking away.

"What?" I needed to know the rest of the sentence, the way Annie would complete him.

But all she said was, "Surprising."

I turned from her, returning to *The Best American*s. They were terrifying there above me, a candy-colored monolith.

"I just want you to be happy," Annie said.

"I am," I said, although *happy* was not it at all. *Doubtful*, maybe, and also *thrilled*. But I couldn't share those words with Annie. She would find them frightening.

"Good," Annie said. "Okay."

She shifted onto her side so we faced each other, a pair of closed parentheses. "Writing group went well," she said.

Writing group. Right. Annie's Saturday meeting, formed through some of her connections at work. I'd met them once, when Annie hosted at our apartment. When she told them about my novel, they all nodded and said, "Interesting!"

"What did they think?" Annie's story must have been up for discussion. I'd helped her with it. A child narrator, a dad, whale watching gone awry. Not the sort of story I would write, but one I could see the shape of and help tug the corners and lines into place.

"Everyone loved the edit you made," she said. "To the end." The edit had been challenging, a slip of authorial vulnerability Annie at first refused to make. After years of reading each other, I knew this tic of hers, how she might focus the story on others as she hid behind the lens. "I sent the story to Elaine." Elaine, her agent.

"Good, Annie," I said. "It's a great story."

"Are you going to send me something soon?" she asked. "What are you working on?"

"I don't know," I said, the truth. Every morning, my alarm went off and sent me to my desk, and I emerged hours later feeling not productive but strange. The writing put me in a stupor, like a drug.

"We're running a generative workshop next Saturday," Annie said. The literary nonprofit ran short creative writing classes. "I could get you a discount."

I had stacks of notebooks piled on my desk, in corners. "I don't think producing stuff is my problem," I said.

"Are you still doing the notebook thing?" I'd started writing longhand after publishing my book. Annie found the process suspicious. It made the writing harder to share. She hadn't seen anything I'd done since Maine.

"I am," I said. The messiness came with a freedom I didn't quite understand, chasing the open feeling I'd found at the residency. Even Annie couldn't read my handwriting.

"Send me something," she insisted. "I miss your writing."

I thought about all those copies of my novel haunting my closet. "Why?" I asked.

"What do you mean, why?" Annie said. "You think about the big things. What you do is different."

"*Interesting*," I said, adding air quotes.

"It really is," Annie said. Annie liked to proclaim that she was a writer of life, and I was a writer of ideas, a way of demonstrating how we complemented each other. She reflected the problems of the world, and I reflected the problems of the mind. I didn't totally know what this meant, except that she often took people from our life and wrote them down with a few details scrambled, while I tried to stay as far away from life as possible. Using anything real made me feel exposed. I'd rather turn my writing cold, manipulated like a machine.

She brushed my hair with her fingers. "You've got an interesting brain."

I thought of what my brain now held. The weekends, the choreographer, Jackie. *I want to know what you want, so I can give it to you.* The way I'd followed my body to him, to this knot of complication, meaning so twisted and coiled that I couldn't see its center.

Annie could take this knot, I knew. She'd straighten the curves, loosen the holds, return everything back to neatness and order. Even as I lay in bed with her, I felt the start of the story press against my mouth, my tongue, ready to pass on to her.

But my jaw tightened, holding everything in. We faced each other, so close we mingled breath. But my silence grew, gaining density until I felt increasingly alone.

I rolled over, sitting up. "This interesting brain needs a snack," I said. 'Do you want anything?"

"No, I'm good," Annie said. She reached for her phone again.

I slipped my sticky, heavy body out from the covers. Our rooms mirrored each other in size and structure. The same weird corners we couldn't fit furniture into, the same-sized bed and desk. We even had the same picture from graduation. Gowned and mortarboarded and flanking Esme, all three of us squinting in the bright sunlight. Sometimes, I forgot that I didn't look like that girl anymore.

"Are you going to be around next weekend?" Annie asked.

On Saturday, the trio would premiere at the festival. "Maybe," I said.

I looked back at her in bed. Deep in her phone. "Night, Annie," I said, then crossed into the common area, leaving her behind.

ON WEDNESDAY, I texted the choreographer that I might not make it out to the Berkshires that weekend. He called right away, an aggressive, old-person move. I ran from my cubicle to answer the call in the bathroom.

"This is important," he said. "I need you."

"But work—" My voice bounced off the tiles.

"I said I needed you, Rabbit." His voice directed in the way of a child, sure but also frightened.

I leaned my elbows hard into my thighs, denting the fabric of my work dress.

"Okay," I said. "I'll be there."

THE DANCE FESTIVAL created its own world there in the mountains, a rustic compound filled by overlapping rounds of access. There were the day-trippers with their one-time passes, bussed in from Pittsfield or New York, the students at the dance school glowing in their workout clothes. There were the teachers, the professionals, the performers, and then finally the donors, each group with their own subcircles nested inside each other. You'd never find just one center, one core.

The choreographer didn't sleep the night before the performance, staying up in the living room to pace and watch over rehearsal videos or lie stock-still on the hardwood floor, mentally running through choreography. Alone in the bed, I tried to sleep, to not be disturbed by his disturbance.

"You're nervous," I said when he finally came into the dark room. My hands found his body, his torso.

"Desperately," he said, tucking his face against my neck.

"I didn't know you got nervous."

"Now you know," he said, wrapping his arms around me. "Now you've learned something new about me."

In the morning, I made whole wheat vegan pancakes, trying to keep the almond milk from curdling or whatever it was that almond milk did. "You didn't eat anything last night," I said, pushing the plate across.

"I can't," he said, not looking at me as he tipped coffee back into his mouth.

He got dressed: black pants, black T-shirt, a strange costume for the mountains in the heat of summer. Then he pulled a pack of cigarettes from a kitchen drawer and went out back to light one.

"You smoke, too?" I asked when he returned.

"Only three times a year," he said.

He gargled with mouthwash and then gathered his keys. Dress rehearsal at the festival.

"What should I wear?" I asked. I'd packed a work dress in my bag, but it looked tweedy now, clashing with his clothes.

"Dress like yourself," he told me, kissing me lightly and leaving the house.

I read for a while, ate lunch, then picked out a stiff gray smock dress with a slight sheen. The skirt hung from my hips like a bell. No earrings, no jewelry. Summery, but austere.

My car struggled up the zigzagging mountain road leading to the festival grounds. A large sign alerted me to the turnoff, taking me up an even steeper hill until I pulled into the parking lot. I found the spot for special guests and hung the choreographer's paper tag on my rearview mirror.

Neat gravel paths wove through the buildings, the bluish stones sharp under the thin soles of my leather sandals. People everywhere, small gatherings filling in the grassy lawns between the theaters and studios. Performers and spectators, I already knew the difference: the latter all eyes, the performers all bodies, flexed tendons and purposeful strides. At regular intervals stood stalls for grilled paninis, pour-over coffee, beer, and wine. Like a county fair, except high culture.

After checking a map pinned up on a board, I followed the path to the main outdoor performance area, the trees parting to reveal a wide and spacious clearing filled with long wooden benches. The grounds sloped down to the white square stage backed by a crest of mountains, perched just on the edge and ready to tip into the green valley. *Worship*, I thought. That's what this place was for, why it had been built.

I spotted the choreographer up by the front. My eyes went right to him as if guided by a signal. I knew he hadn't slept at all, but he didn't look tired. He looked perfect, golden.

I made my way through the crowd toward him. "There you are," he said, hand on my back, kissing me. "The wolves are here. Are you ready?"

"What do you mean?" I asked, and then a man in a short-sleeved button-down appeared, hand out, waiting to be greeted.

"I haven't seen you since Paris," said the man, shaking the choreographer's hand. "Can't wait to see the new work." And then his eyes drifted to me. "Who's this?"

The choreographer placed his palm on the small of my back. I couldn't tell if the gesture was meant to steer or reassure. "My partner," he explained.

So many hands to shake, smiles to match, people hungry for the choreographer. I grinned and greeted like I knew what I was doing. By his side, my presence continued to be explained: *my partner, my partner, my partner.*

When it was time to sit, everyone knew, like church. And then the talking was done, a moment of silence, all of us alone yet merged in the same shared experience.

Here, the dancers couldn't hide in the artificial dark of an indoor theater. We watched them climb from the back stairs and find their marks. They wore flexible white jumpsuits, just a few strips of thin fabric tied across their chests. Jackie's straps must have been taped into place. Her hair had been plastered into a tight, round topknot, so that from a distance the dancers appeared genderless, simply three incredible bodies.

They froze at their spots, returned to Grecian statues. I held my breath, felt everyone around me holding their breath, all of us waiting for the music to snap the dancers into life.

The trio could have lasted six minutes. Eight. I didn't know, because I slipped out of time, watching the three people I'd just shared company with turn into pure energy and motion. They shifted and swung each other, lifting and rolling, and though I didn't know the right words, the vocabulary, I understood what they were doing.

Jackie's early movements involved long, static holds and stillness, her body a bridge and a pivot point between the two male dancers. Swinging and arching between them, their joint force tugged her through the space of the stage. But then she stopped, expanded. Her movement overwhelmed them, their bodies and gestures an extension of hers. Melded, combined, their shared power lifted into the clear mountain air, taking all the force from the seemingly limitless space. I stopped breathing for a moment, tuned into the heat of the choreographer beside me.

At the end, I stood with everyone. I clapped. Then I turned to him and said, "That was wonderful."

We stopped clapping before everyone else, alone in the applause. "Thank you," he said, kissing my forehead.

There was more to watch, then more mingling, congratulating the flushed dancers who had been returned to their mortal selves, slick with sweat and panting.

"You were great," I said. They smiled and laughed, full of adrenaline mixed with the joy of a completed performance. "That was really great."

TJ and Zac both thanked me, hugging me at once. Jackie stood apart, her chest still heaving, her feet bleeding between her toes. "Thanks," she said, and I looked at her bare torso for a beat too long.

"Great work, you three," the choreographer said, slapping them on their backs like a baseball coach. "Have a good time tonight."

Then he took my hand and led me away, my skin still damp from the boys' sweat.

That evening, I went with the choreographer to a private dinner at the festival director's cabin, really a rustic palace, one of the inner sanctums. During the meal, I sat by the choreographer's side at a long table, and someone blessedly fed me grilled chicken. Everyone talked the same way the performers had danced, light with quick twists, hardly letting the words land.

"Where did you find her?" asked an ambient composer named Ron, pointing his fork at me. I braced myself for more of this, of being talked about in the third person.

"Maine," said the choreographer. He put his hand on the back of my chair. "I pulled her out of the sea."

"We were inland," I said, and the grumpy tone of my delivery hit just right, making the table laugh.

After the meal, the party opened up onto the lawn and more people arrived, the ones who hadn't been invited to dinner. Giant speakers blasted over an outdoor dance floor as an open bar poured over us, the strings of lights bathing the rural forest in soothing, artificial day.

I spotted Franny from afar, already sloshed, pointing at me and shouting, "Wellesley!" and Jackie, who'd changed into a white party dress, her long hair down and set off by sparkling chain earrings. Her lean arms guided a gawky man in a suit out onto the dance floor. Clearly a donor, I thought, looking at him. An event like this, I realized, was probably where the choreographer had met his ex-wife.

Everyone seemed blessed with ethereal beauty. Bodies moved on the dance floor like they were made of air, colored in temporarily so we mortals could view them. I stood in wonder, an outsider briefly allowed into the realm of more beguiling spirits.

At first, the choreographer steered me through the crowd, finding those he liked and giving out real, wide-armed hugs. *Here she is*, he seemed to say as he pushed me forward, presenting me to his world. They took my hands, my arms, assessing my textures, my youth. A human changeling, a creature of the earth. Then, once I'd been absorbed, they turned back to him, my presence more or less forgotten.

Still, the choreographer's happiness radiated all the way inside of me so that I mistook it for my own. I watched him open and relax, his beauty amplified, filling me with affection and pleasure, even if he still talked too much during dinner.

His grip loosened on me so I could set him free through the party. I drank seltzer—clearly, I would be driving—and drifted to the edges, trying to absorb everything. He stood with a group, laughing, and I knew I could leave him, walking out of the light.

I went behind the house to look at the huge field full of fireflies, dipping and clinging to grass still warm from the day. At the other end stood shadowy humps, goats chewing in the dark.

"I found you."

He'd left the light, his figure clear to me even in shadowed silhouette. His limbs hung with an unusual heaviness, his gait just an edge unsteady. He was drunk.

"You're drunk," I said.

"Indeed." He looked inside his empty plastic cup, then threw it in the grass.

"You're littering."

"Who cares?"

He stood over me, and I felt, as I rarely did, how much taller he was than me, how much stronger. His sloppy-drunk hands touched my hair, my cheek. "You'll tell me if something's not okay, Rabbit?"

"You really need to think about eating simple carbohydrates again," I told him, but he was pulling my hair down, guiding me toward the wall of the house where there weren't any windows.

"You really liked it?" he said.

"I told you, it's wonderful."

"And did you like Jackie?"

I froze as if with fright, but fright mixed with a pulse, a sudden shivering along my skin.

Before I could move, he grabbed my wrists. "What are you doing?" I said, tugging, but his hands were too strong. *He could crush me*, I thought, heartbeat up, the skin-pulse turning into a throbbing.

"Do you like the way she looks tonight?" And I was up against the wall, nowhere to go. *You can tell him this isn't okay*, I thought, but I didn't. I didn't know what it was.

"What would you like her to do to you?" he asked. "Would you like her to kiss you?"

And he leaned down and kissed me, not with his mouth, but with hers, soft and assertive. "Would you like her to touch you?" He let go of my hands to brush my hair, my cheek, the gestures cloying as he unbuttoned the top of my dress. Still, I felt lit up, his hand tracing new lines of electricity along me.

He knelt on the ground in front of me, pulling down my underwear and gripping my hips. "How about this?" And then I was stuffing my hands in my mouth, trying to shut myself up with the sounds of the party just behind me.

He emerged, replacing his mouth with his hand, the fingers slipping into me tenderly. "How is she doing?" he asked, and I groaned into my palm. He laughed and said, "She'd probably be rougher than this." He drove harder up into me, pinning my low back to the wall. "She'd probably try too hard. Be a little much."

I threw my arms around him as I came, crying out. I didn't care if anybody heard. The darkness took me, the emptiness pushed and stretched until it held us both inside.

The wall kept me up as I returned to myself, crucial support for my jellied body. The choreographer brushed my hair back behind my ears. "How did she do?" he asked. I stared. He'd returned to himself, his touch his own again. "You look blank. She must have done well."

He buttoned up my dress and handed over my underwear, kissing me. "When you're ready, put those on," he told me. "We've got a party to get back to."

THE NEXT MORNING, I felt him leave the bed and walk into the kitchen. Eyes still closed, I listened to him fill a glass with water from the faucet. "I'm hungover," he announced.

"I'm not surprised," I said. I got up to make coffee, joining him in the kitchen. He stood hunched over the sink, hands braced against the counter. He didn't look hungover. He still looked annoyingly glorious.

"I think you're right," he said. "I think I need to eat carbs before I drink."

"I told you," I said. "I warned you about this new diet thing." I kissed the wing of his shoulder blade before moving on to search for coffee beans.

He watched me walk around the kitchen. "Rabbit."

I stopped, my stomach hollowing. I felt fragile, suddenly destructible.

"Last night, at the party, I—"

He stopped talking, his mouth still open as if he'd run out of words.

I turned to him. "What was that?" I asked.

"I don't know," he said. "I—was it okay?"

The hollowness filled with me again, and I kept going, taking the beans down from the shelf.

"I'm fine," I said. "I'm okay."

I ground the beans. I poured the water.

What I didn't say: *It was wonderful.*

Chapter Seven

With fall came the professors, the students, my days filled with Excel spreadsheets and printing syllabi and loading PowerPoint presentations from thumb drives into smart podiums. I still woke up at five A.M. each weekday, but the hour got darker, felt earlier, the words dripping out like thickened paint.

I thought I'd wean myself off the choreographer a bit, but then I'd get it again, that all-skin hunger, and I'd buy a train ticket to New York at outrageous cost or drive out to meet him in the mountains, the trees along the highway turning the colors of Skittles.

One day, I brought my bike to work so I could ride to Brookline afterward for a reading. Rebecca, the other writer at the Maine residency, had just published a book of lyric ecopoetry, and she'd come down from her home in southern Vermont to do a brief tour.

Wrapped in rich layers of unnecessary textiles, she read slowly, her heavy syntax filled with scenes I recognized from Maine. The blush of leaves, the crunch of stones as I walked up the path to my studio. Crisp fall, clean air, the lush dying of summer splendor.

I mingled in the basement reading space afterward, talking to people I knew: the bookstore's buyer, other writers, the web of semiprofessionals who made up the Boston literary world.

"How's writing going?" asked the buyer.

I tried not to think about how the bookstore did not stock my book. "It's good," I said. "You know, slow. Getting up early in the morning."

"That's how I work, too," she said. "And how's Annie?" Everyone seemed to know Annie.

"Great, as always," I said.

"Say hi to her for me," said the buyer. "I owe her tea."

Rebecca signed her last book and found me, greeting me with a warm hug scented like rich incense. At the residency, she'd taken something of a maternal stance toward me, offering frequent advice during our lake walks.

"I'm so glad you could make it," she said. "I read your book. So different!"

The buyer shuttled off the folding chairs, and the reading's leftovers trickled to a dimly lit underground bar next door. Slumped and nervous, we talked to each other at uncomfortable distances, shouting to be heard.

Rebecca and I shared an order of truffle fries, standing together at the bar. "Have you kept up with anyone else from Maine?" she asked.

"Actually, I have," I said. "Do you remember the dance guy?"

She laughed. "Oh my god, that guy."

"Yeah. We're sort of dating."

She put down the fry she'd just picked up. "Really?" I'd expected her to be surprised, but not that surprised. "For how long?"

"I'm not sure, actually. Since spring." When should I have started counting? The first time in New York?

Her great brows began to stretch and twitch as if they alone were digesting the information. "Wow."

"You're stunned," I said.

She turned her torso to the bar. "He is my age and you're . . . not," she said.

"I know. I'm aware."

She picked the fry up again, ate it, then gathered a few more.

"I'm not surprised by him," she said. "He definitely had his eye on you." My skin heated. "But . . . aren't you queer?" She said the last word with barely any breath or force, as if it might have suddenly reverted back to being a slur.

"I am," I said. "I date cis men, too."

She turned away again. Her face couldn't hide any of her brain's internal conflict, the structures distending again as she struggled to locate this new knowledge about me.

"Is it just that you thought I didn't date men, or is this something with him specifically?" I asked.

"If you want the truth, him specifically."

"He's different out here," I said.

"I'm sure. We all are."

She gave me the sort of look that wraps you in comfort just before a whispered warning. My mother looked at me that way, and Rebecca probably used the same expression with her own teenage daughters. "He's very successful," she said.

"That's not—I'm not dating him for money, or anything," I said, throat tight, annoyed perhaps because I was more dazzled by his material world than I liked to admit.

"I know, of course not," she said. "But have you ever dated a powerful man like that?"

"No," I said. My male partners until that point had been firm betas, quick to roll onto their backs and reveal their passing knowledge of gender studies.

Rebecca continued to hog the fries, quenching the salt with her beer. "I thought so," she said. "You don't seem like you would. You don't seem like you'd put up with it."

I tried to ask more, but she shifted the conversation back to her book, the great success of her summer tomatoes, passing me on to other conversations until I'd had enough. Settling up, I left the bar and started the long bike ride home.

The Korean restaurants of Allston flashed past me as I filtered and dodged through the cars, crossing back over the dark river. Rebecca's words bounced around as if tossed and stirred by each pothole. *Queer. You don't seem like you'd put up with it*. Like rocks, they knocked holes into the image I had of myself, the woman I used to be.

She's wrong, I thought, pedaling through Harvard Square and bombing down the Cambridge Street tunnel. But as my thighs began to ache on the push up the hill, I remembered the grip of his hands on my wrist, fright mixed with an unknown thrill. And my body, responding like an obedient dog, chasing him all around the East Coast.

At home, I found Annie on the couch, eating a bowl of pasta and vegetables while watching a cooking show on her laptop.

"Hey," I said. "I thought you had a second date with Mohawk–Septum Piercing." As a rule, I did not learn the names of Annie's suitors until date four or five.

Annie made an exaggerated sad face. "She flaked on me."

"Boo." I dropped my backpack and hung up my helmet. The food smelled good—I'd burned through the fries, their calories insufficient. "Can I take a bowl?"

"Of course."

I spooned myself some pasta and joined her on the couch. We often ate dinner side by side like this, ignoring our perfectly serviceable table.

"Did you reschedule?" I asked.

"No," Annie said, spearing a noodle. "She said she doesn't think it's going to work out. She's still hung up on her ex."

"Boo," I repeated. "At least she was honest with you."

"I guess." She stacked her fork with multiple sad and wrinkly summer squashes from the Market Basket. "We didn't even get to really make out."

The contestants on the cooking show ran around, panicked and shouting. "It's better to know now," I told her. "Before you get too involved."

She stuck her bare feet on the coffee table. Her red toenail polish had chipped. "Yeah. You're right." She filled her cheeks with air, letting it out in one puff. "How was the reading? You get to catch up with your camp friend?" Annie called the Maine residency "camp," a diminutive cuteness, even though she had pushed me to apply in the first place. She wanted us to go together, but when the decisions came back she had been waitlisted. A new crack opened between us, slender but still perceptible. Annie knew the director. Annie usually got into these sorts of things.

"I did," I said, chewing a mushy noodle. She had slightly overcooked them. "It was nice."

"You tell her your news?" Annie, I noticed, often avoided referring to the choreographer directly.

The vegetables needed salt, too. "Yeah," I said. "She seemed surprised."

"Why?"

"I don't think she thought I dated men," I said, picking my answer. Annie didn't say anything at first, making what I called one of her "grumpy dog" sounds.

She took her time spearing more noodles. "Do you remember how much you complained about him? When you were gone?" She chewed with her back teeth, her cheek puffed out. "I didn't think you liked him at all."

At the residency, I would climb up the hill to hunt for enough reception to call Annie, stretching out on a cold rock during our long talks. But on the phone, our new awkwardness continued to expand. The residency's rejection of Annie had surprised me as much as my own acceptance. "Camp" hadn't even been my idea—I was just following Annie.

My arrival at the lush property had stirred fresh guilt as I settled into Annie's spot, the place she probably would have been offered if I had not applied. But alone in my cabin I also felt thrilled. No one at the residency knew me.

So when I called Annie, I focused on the negatives. Mostly, the choreographer. I said things like *If only you were here*. I didn't talk about the time and focus and pleasure, the way the writing cracked open so I could surrender and settle inside. The quiet of my cabin, my desk, my work totems, John Cage's *10 Rules for Students and Teachers* pinned at eye level. A fresh loosening of my neck and shoulders, the writing itself taking on a new pliancy.

And then long walks in the clean, cold air, the stretch of freshwater beside me.

He had his eye on you.

"I did," I acknowledged. "He annoyed me."

"What changed?"

I knew what Annie wanted: a narrative, a pattern of elegantly spaced beats between "bad" and "good" to vindicate both my attitude then and how I felt about the choreographer now. A clear line showing cause and effect. But I couldn't find an arc or a scene, nothing to explain it. Just a chemical shift so subtle I hadn't really noticed.

"I'm not sure," I said.

She scraped the powdered cheese with the edge of her fork. "You're a little different, when you come back," she said.

"What do you mean?" I said. "When I come back from being with him?"

She nodded.

"How so?"

She stuck a granule of parmesan on the end of a fork tine. "A little hazier, I guess," she said. "Quiet."

She licked the fork. "I'm usually just tired," I said.

"I know," she said.

She looked at my socked feet resting on the coffee table, a hole emerging over my right big toe. "I can't imagine what you're like with him," she said. "It's like with Sheila."

"You hated Sheila," I said.

"Because she hurt you," Annie said.

Sheila, my grad school ex. She'd dumped me at the end of my last semester, right before I was supposed to move into her apartment in Northampton. The breakup had been uniquely devastating, shattering the foundation on which I'd built last two years of my life. Annie drove out from Boston and put me back together. She made sure I ate and showered and sat in the library until my thesis had been produced. *Come back to Boston,* Annie had said. *We'll have a beautiful life.*

On the screen, a beautiful woman tried a bite of food, then said a scathing remark.

Annie propped her elbow up on the back of the couch so she fully faced me. "And he's a man," she said.

"I'm aware." The words came out more defensively than I'd intended. Annie's face flickered, under attack. "I get your worry," I said more softly. How all the things the choreographer contained—*man* and *older* and *prestige*—expanded his capacity for damage.

"I just want you to be happy," she said.

Happy. Even just the edge of the choreographer in my mind could drop the bottom out of me. Not *happy*, but *want*, a true but imprecise substitution.

We tidied up, washing our dishes in the kitchen, the leftovers parceled out into lunch-sized Tupperware containers. "Tell me about your weekend," Annie said.

The sun on the water, a trail bloodied with red leaves, bedsheets, and an unsatisfying treat of vegan apple cider donuts. A moment when he'd breathed open-mouthed into my hair, desperate to inhale me. I could present these scenes, but knew already how Annie would mark them. *What do you mean here? What are you doing? I need a broader context.*

"It was nice," I said. "It was fall."

Annie's hand touched my shoulder, intending a soft gesture, but her fingers felt muscular and hard. "It's okay," she said, but

I hadn't experienced my short statements as failures. What Annie wanted from me, I realized, was the same thing she wanted from the work. Clear statements, legibility. Some sign or signal, something like safety or protection.

I yawned, bringing a sudsy hand to my open mouth. "It's late for you," Annie said.

The reading had kept me up. "I know," I said, rinsing off my hands. "I'll be fine."

Annie smiled at me with a proud expression I suddenly didn't want. Was this all I was good for? A tortoise plodding forward. Diligence and rigor. Service and time. I didn't know how to do anything different.

I said good night, shutting myself in my room. Unlike Annie, my desk was covered in sloppy detritus. Books and notebooks, piles of rocks and a melted stub of candlewax. Where Annie had her vision board, a rotating cast of logos and sunlight, I had the simple John Cage printout and a black-and-white post-card showing a woman in profile with her hair draped over her face.

Since returning from Maine, I'd fallen into a kind of murki-ness. Each morning, I listened to Annie make coffee and breakfast while I drifted through the writing, tracing some thin barrier keeping me from the work. I knew I was only waiting, on the edge of the same break I'd felt in Maine. The loosening, the pleasure of being pulled under.

I left the notebook open on the table and changed into an old T-shirt and sweatpants. My room, my belongings. The bookshelf I'd found and painted teal, all streaked and glopped from lack of skill. The framed photograph of me and Esme and Annie at graduation, another of my family, a print I'd bought at a craft fair that showed plants blooming from the rotund bodies of women. Everything stamped with my own life, my name. Nothing resembled the life of the choreographer, said *partner* or *lover* or *Rabbit*.

I got in bed with a book, but even as I read alone, I felt him there, fresh want flooding my skin like drink.

ONE FRIDAY EVENING, I boarded the train for New York and settled in for a few long hours of bad Wi-Fi and lukewarm dining car sandwiches, an experience that became much worse when we stopped just outside New Rochelle and did not move for thirty minutes. A Metro North train blocked the platform, stuck due to electrical problems.

I tried to stream something relaxing, tethering my laptop to my phone, when an email alert flagged across the top right corner of my screen. An address I didn't recognize, with a professional-sounding domain.

A woman at a boutique literary agency had read my book and enjoyed it. I was surprised. The distributor had recently emailed me that they needed the space and would be pulping my copies unless I paid for media mail from California.

The agent was curious about my state of representation. I should email her to meet, if I was ever in New York.

I jolted as the lights flickered, the train's engine engaging. The electrical problem had been solved, and now we glided smoothly into the city.

"Tell her you'll have lunch on Monday," the choreographer told me as we sat down for a late dinner in his apartment. Grain bowl for him, *cacio e pepe* for me.

"I have work," I said.

"Tell them you're sick."

The first thought I had was that someone might get locked out of their university email. The excuse was so sad, I didn't say it.

He knew, though. "Do you want to write," he said, "or help professors find their glasses?"

"My parents are academics," I told him. "Finding glasses is what I was born to do."

Still, I emailed back, called out of work, then spent the weekend reading free-access stories on lit journal websites, trying to think of intelligent things to say. The choreographer fed me coffee and then laid down on the living room floor, planning moves for a new solo.

At one point, I looked away from my computer to where he lay on the ground. His arms and legs were straight and stiff. He looked rigid but pulsing, the air buzzing with his internal vibrations.

When he was done, I heard a little drop, an exhalation. His hands relaxed on his stomach, his feet drooped to the side like in corpse pose.

I got up and stood over him. He looked tired, just barely back in the world.

"Can I lie down next to you?" I asked. He blinked, then nodded.

I curled up against him, my cheek pressed to his chest. His heart thudded beneath me, accelerated with imagined exertions. Alone as a child in bed, I couldn't believe that one day I might lie close enough to hear another person's heartbeat. That it would pump just alongside my ear, sounding like mine. Even more miraculous, that it wouldn't be, near but still outside.

★　★　★

ON MONDAY, I left the choreographer's apartment with my duffel bag, heading to the restaurant early with the intention of stashing it under the chair before the agent got there. But she'd already arrived.

"Hi," she said, standing up and shaking my hand firmly.

"Hi," I said, and then we both stood there for a moment, forgetting to sit.

She was young, what I now thought of as dancer-young, but hid her youth with large glasses and a shirt buttoned all the way up to her neck.

"I'm glad this worked out," she said. "What excellent timing."

"I know," I said. "It's spooky."

We finally sat. I looked at the menu. Too many options, too many types of coffees. "So you read my book?" I said.

Books. She looked relieved. "I did," she said. "It was very exciting."

Finally, something other than "different." "I'm glad you feel that way," I said. "This might be the wrong question, but how did you find it?"

"It came across my desk."

"Wow," I said. "It just walked across, huh?"

She did not laugh. "My boss gave it to me," she said. "She doesn't have room for any other clients, but she thinks we might be a good fit."

"Oh," I said. I felt hot, flushed. "That's great. What did you like about it?"

"Your energy and voice," the agent said. "If I'd worked on it, I might have pushed you more on the plot. It's a bit cerebral, heady. But I liked where you were going."

I picked at the corner of the menu with my nail. "That's good," I said. "That sounds like we might be a good fit."

By the end of lunch, I'd signed a contract that could be eliminated at any time while she charged the meal to the agency.

On the train, I texted the choreographer, and he called back immediately with congratulations.

"That's fantastic," he said.

"It's a little bit hard to believe." I had the contract in front of me. The words *acts of God* appeared for some reason.

"Not for me. I knew they'd love it."

The last word did it, the tiny *it*. Not *you*, but an object, a thing.

My book.

"You," I said.

He went quiet.

"You did this," I said. "You sent them my book, didn't you?"

"Rabbit—"

"And the timing." I thought about him at the residency again. A bad puppet. Preferred to run the show. "Did you tell them when I was going to be in New York?"

He said a lot of things. The head agent's daughter took classes at his dance school. They started to talk. "I was just trying to help."

"No," I said, gripping the phone. "You were *investing*."

I hung up the phone and set it to Airplane Mode.

I turned it back on outside New Haven. A call from the choreographer immediately came through.

"So what if I am?" he said. "You don't think you're worth investing in?"

"Not by you," I said. "I'm fucking you." My seatmate, a long-haired woman in a business suit, twitched.

"All the more reason. I'm a very interested stakeholder."

"Is that it? You just want to be able to take me to parties and say 'My partner, the writer' instead of 'My partner, the office drudge'?"

"I don't care what you are," he said, his voice starting to match my bite. "*You* care what you are. I just want to see you happy."

"You don't want to see me fail."

"I'd love to see you fail," he said, "because then you would finally be taking a risk."

"Fuck you!" I hung up again and kept the phone on Airplane Mode until we pulled into Providence.

I called the choreographer. "I'm keeping the agent."

"Good," he said. "And are you going to keep me?"

"Back Bay!" shouted the conductor. He walked through the aisle, tugging tickets out from under the metal tabs. "Next stop, Back Bay, last stop, South Station."

"Yes," I said. "But don't do that again."

When we pulled into South Station, my seatmate stood up. "Good luck," she said, and walked away before the train had come to a complete halt.

"I DON'T KNOW," Annie said over her coffee. "Isn't it a little fucked up that he didn't tell you? That he sent the book without your consent?"

I'd taken the weekend off from the choreographer. Partly because of the agent thing, and also because earlier that week, I'd heard a thump and screech from Annie's side of the apartment. She'd thrown a shoe at the wall, a soft one at least, but the sole still left a dark scuff on the paint. "They said no," she explained, slumping onto the floor with her back against the bed. Her agent had sent the whale-watching story off to one of the big glossies, a major magazine whose logo Annie had recently added to her vision board.

"I was so close," she continued.

"Annie, that's great. That's amazing," I said, sitting on the ground with her. "Not everyone gets so close. You were in the running." But she just stared at her knees and said, "When is it ever going to be my day?"

When I'd explained to the choreographer why I needed to stay in Somerville, he said he understood. But he also said, "We get rejected all the time." And I felt strange, hearing that *we*, as if the two of us belonged to one artistic species.

"Easy for you to say," I said, "from your position."

"True," he acknowledged, "but how do you think I got here."

With help, I thought. *With her, the ex-wife.* But I didn't say anything, letting his words fill the space and crevices between us.

That Saturday was Fluff Fest, the neighborhood celebration of marshmallow spread, and I spent the morning wandering with Annie through the crowd, eating crepes stuffed with the sweet pearlescent substance. We went each year, but this time I felt a new annoyance at all the people, a mass of moving distraction.

Still buzzed from sugar, we camped out at our favorite coffee shop, snagging a coveted outdoor table. People packed the courtyard to soak in the last of the fall sunlight.

"It just seems sneaky," Annie said, continuing the conversation about the agent.

I sipped my coffee. "Maybe," I said. Even though I'd been mad, I now felt the surprising urge to defend him, or to at least complicate things. "But the book's published. It's out there. It's not like I was keeping it a secret."

"Why didn't he ask first, then?"

And I knew, right away. "I would have said no," I said. "I would have refused the help."

"Because you have principles," Annie said. "You wouldn't take help from your boyfriend."

"Right." But my principles would have meant no agent.

"Are you going to keep her?"

I hadn't expected the question. "I think so," I said. "Why not?" Annie's own agent had come through her coworker at the literary nonprofit.

"Sure," said Annie. But her expression twisted then clamped, the light wisp of judgment. "Whatever's best for you."

She turned away, focusing back on her laptop. She was supposed to be working on her novel, but I could see a blue ribbon of posts reflected in her irises. "Did you like my book?" I asked. My voice sounded small.

"What?" She tilted the laptop screen down to look at me. "Of course."

"Did you ever think of showing it to your agent?" I said.

She wiped a croissant crumb from the corner of her mouth. "You never asked."

"It's awkward," I said.

"Sure," Annie said. Her eyes avoided me. "But you didn't seem like you needed all that. You had your friend with their press. And experimental stuff isn't really Elaine's thing."

I looked away and sipped my drink. The coffee had cooled quickly in the chill. I leaned away, my back against the chair.

She reached out to close the distance, grabbing my hand. "Hey, you know I like your stuff," Annie said. "I'm always trying to help."

"I know," I said. But I felt an odd buzzing just under my skin. *All that.* Why did Annie need it, and not me?

"We're good?" she said.

I suddenly wanted her hand off me. I didn't like the feel of her skin. "Yeah, we're good," I said.

Annie squeezed my fingers, then looked back at her laptop, pushing the screen upright. I held my book, *The Complete Short Stories of Leonora Carrington*, but kept passing my eyes over the same paragraph.

"Want to see the mock-ups of my new office?" Annie asked. The literary nonprofit planned to move to a new building by the harbor. She turned the laptop around so I could see computer-generated pictures of an open, airy room, the huge glass walls looking out onto the water.

"Nice," I said.

"And down here is the new event space," she said, switching to the next slide. "We'll be able to hold bigger crowds."

I stared at an auditorium filled with faceless cartoon avatars. "Cool," I said.

The young, cute barista with the shaved head stepped onto the patio carrying a chocolate muffin on a thin white saucer. "Oh, no, we didn't order that," I said as she put the baked good in front of me. She smelled like sandalwood, her bare arms covered in snaking botanical tattoos.

"It's on the house," she said, winking, then turned to go back inside. When I picked up the plate, I found a piece of paper underneath with her phone number and a smiley face.

"How does this happen to me?" I said, staring at the doodle.

"Fall's your good season," Annie said. She reached across the table to take a pinch of muffin. "She's cute. Are you going to call her?"

I felt the choreographer's fingers on my cheek. His voice. *Would you like her to touch you?* "I'm not sure if I can," I said.

"Because of him?" Annie said.

I tried to spy the barista through the glare of the coffee shop windows. Was she really as cute as I thought? "Yes," I said, "because of him."

I TEXTED THE choreographer that I needed to talk, even though he'd told me to stop texting before I called him.

"Is everything okay?" He still sounded worried about the agent thing.

Sitting on my bed, I looked out my window at the bright fall leaves. "Yeah," I said. "This isn't about . . . I wanted to tell you something."

But then the words got stuck in me, leaving me staring at my knees.

"Yes?"

"I went to the coffee shop," I said. "And the uh, barista gave me her number."

More quiet on the other end. I tried to imagine him in his apartment, what his face looked like.

"How did she do it? How did she know?"

"She brought me a muffin. Maybe my Somerville Pride pin? I don't know."

"Do you like her?"

"I haven't really talked to her."

"I mean . . . do you find her attractive."

I should have forced him to FaceTime, even though he hated video calls. He'd cleaned his voice again. I had no idea what he was thinking.

"Yeah," I said. "I mean, I think she's cute."

I could hear myself breathing through the static of the phone.

"Do you want to call her?"

"I don't know." I got up and started pacing around the confines of my bedroom. "I don't want to—I mean, I know there's us."

"Rabbit." I stopped. His voice felt like a grip on the back of my neck, the light pressure signaling the importance of what he was about to say. "Are you going to call her?"

I swallowed, a gritty feeling in my throat. I didn't seem to have any liquid left in my body. "Do you want me to?" I asked.

I heard his voice as low and clear as if he spoke directly in my ear. "Yes."

ANNIE WATCHED FROM my bedroom door as I got ready for the date. "What do you think?" I asked her. I'd braided my hair and dressed in black jeans and a jacket, just a touch of gold from the thick hoops in my ears.

"I'd vamp up a bit," Annie said. "Do the Sylvia Plath lipstick."

Digging out my makeup bag, I obeyed, flicking dark wings of liquid eyeliner and smearing the purplish-pink cream on my lips.

"There you go." Annie approved. She stepped close, adjusting my collar. "You nervous?"

I fixed a pin in my hair. We stood side by side in the mirror. Although I'd worn these clothes hundreds of times, my reflection had a gloss of unfamiliarity. She looked harder, this version of me, the emphasis of the makeup exerting a brittle clarity.

"Maybe," I said.

I'd suggested a bicycle date. Bicycle dates meant no talking, just bodies gliding around each other on wheeled frames as we tested each other's speed and daring. Sometimes I rode ahead, sometime she did, sometimes we took up the whole damn street, daring the cars to hit us.

The cool fall day turned too warm as we rode up the Mystic River, taking a path sandwiched between the highway and the muddy, swan-filled water. The barista pedaled fast and hard, her wide hips powering the metal frame up the hills and over the bridges. I kept my eyes on her, panting, watching her stand to bear down on the pedals with her weight.

At a red light, she took off her denim jacket and tied it around her waist. Passing close, I studied the rest of her floral tattoos. Yarrow, horsetail, lavender.

"I like your tattoos," I told her.

She smiled, her teeth straight and white. "Thanks."

We swung around and returned to Somerville, watching the sunset from the base of the Prospect Hill tower. The light turned thick and golden as it settled on the churchlike spires of Harvard, the glass towers of Boston.

"I'm exhausted," I said. Our fingers touched as I passed back the spliff. Even the tips of her fingers felt warm and soft. "You're hard to keep up with."

"I know," she said. "I like to go fast."

I leaned back against the stone tower, shifting my shoulder close to her. I liked her smell, her earthy physicality. I could see her in my life immediately. How easily she'd get along with Annie, how I could hang around the coffee shop writing as I waited for her to get off work. She matched the life I'd planned so well that I started slipping into it with ease. Someone my age, a woman, already in my world.

She liked her coworkers; she liked baking. She loved animals and volunteered at the exotic animal refuge outside Worcester. "And I got a new puppy," she said. "Do you want to see her?" On her phone she scrolled through pictures of a sweet blue pittie nestled in her lap. The dog's square face summoned odd cooing sounds from my mouth.

"I love dogs," I said. I passed back the phone and the last of the spliff. "But we can't have animals in our building." Also, I spent most weekends out of town, fucking the choreographer.

"You'll have to come by and meet Fiona, then," said the barista. "I'll make you dinner. I'm going to slow roast pork shoulder soon. You eat meat, right?"

"Mm-hmm," I said, nodding.

I could tell she had to make herself not look at me. This left me free to look at her—the swoop of her neck, the width of her mouth. "I want to kiss you," I told her. I felt the urge like a slight, questioning nudge.

She stubbed out the spliff, hugging her knees in with a grin. "I think I'd like that."

But then I felt him, the choreographer, pulsing inside me. He breathed through all the miles and distance. *Would you like her to kiss you?*

"But I have to tell you—I'm with someone." His presence pushed on my neck, my chest, a flutter of blood and movement. "He knows. I mean he's okay with this. He's a man. Cisgender."

She dimmed briefly, like a cloud passing over the sun. "So you're poly? And bi?"

"Yeah, that's it."

Her light returned, the words slotting me back into recognizability. "That's fine. You can still kiss me."

I leaned forward to close the gap between us, my hand going to her cheek, her jaw. But the closer I drew, the stronger it felt, like déjà vu. Not my own force propelling me toward the barista, but a pressure on my neck, a presence. As our lips touched, I felt him, there. Not me kissing her, but the choreographer.

I pulled back to look at her. She smiled.

"That was nice," she said.

"Yes," I said, touching the back of my neck. "Great."

After the date, I biked alone back to my apartment. Annie wasn't home, off at some panel, some work event. Still, I closed the door to my bedroom before calling him.

"I went on a date with her," I said. "I just got back."

"Oh." I could hear a siren roaring on his end, imagined him standing by his windows. "How was it?"

"It was nice."

"Just nice?"

I stood by my own window, tugging the gold hoop in my ear. "We kissed."

"Did you kiss her or did she kiss you?"

"I did it. I kissed her."

"I imagine that's how it is," he said. "I imagine you take the lead with them. I bet you're in control."

I pressed the phone screen hard to my ear, as if trying to imprint the ridges against it. "Not like with you," I said.

He didn't say anything. I heard the siren glide away.

"Your roommate's away next weekend?" he said. Annie had a conference in Denver.

"Yes," I said.

"Good," he said. "I'll see you then."

BEFORE LEAVING FOR Colorado, Annie grilled me on the date. "She seems nice," Annie said as we ate dinner on the couch. We'd made chicken cacciatore poured over a bed of polenta, the yellow corn heavily creamed.

"Nice isn't really a quality," I said.

Annie frowned, sticking out her lower lip. "She's really cute, you jerk," she said. She kicked my knee lightly with a socked foot.

"I know she is."

"Why haven't you called her, then?"

"It's been *two days*," I said.

"I know, I know." She cut into the tender meat with the side of her fork. "I'm just really excited for you."

I did not feel excited. I was back up in my head and tearing myself into bits. I avoided the coffee shop, brewing my own at home and carrying it down the hill to work in my insulated mug. *Saving money*, I congratulated myself.

During the week, he called a couple of times. We didn't talk about the date again. The barista texted me, too, mostly just *I had a nice time* and pictures of Fiona the rescue dog. I replied with the heart-eyes emoji. She sent back the emoji giving a side kiss.

When I met the choreographer on the street with the visitor parking pass, I knew right away that something was off. He held his body tight and tense, sparking with unusual charge. His kiss on my cheek felt dry and distant, his eyes not really looking at me.

But as soon as we were inside my apartment, he was on me, his lips pressing hard as he pushed me toward the bedroom. He began to fuck me right away, and for the first time I felt he wasn't fucking me but a near approximation, pounding hard into my body. He had me flat on my stomach, and as he fucked, he took my left wrist and pinned it to the bed. "Stop," I said. "Stop it, you're hurting me."

He pulled off immediately, stepping back to the other side of the room. I sat up and turned to face him. "What are you doing?" I said. My wrist still tingled from the burn of skin on skin, and I kept my right hand around it like a bracelet.

The choreographer breathed deeply, taking control of himself before sitting down at my desk. "I'm sorry," he said. "I keep thinking about your barista."

He wouldn't look at me. "Why did you tell me to call her?" I asked.

The more uncomfortable he felt, the more composed he became, like he planned to rebuild himself from the outside in.

"I want you to have what you want," he said, looking at me.

And I wanted him then, a wave that spread across my limbs, unsettling the structures deep inside me. My wrist still tingled, and I liked it. I wanted to crawl to him, sit at his feet and surrender. Let him do what he wanted to me.

Fright quickly followed. I'd never felt the wish to give myself up in such a way. *You don't want that*, I told myself, staying on the bed.

"You can say you're jealous."

"Can I?" he said. "I can't meet that part of you. Not fully."

I remembered the dance festival, Jackie, the lift of my heart as I realized he could crush me. My wrist still burned, a new door opening.

"No, you can't," I said. "That side of me gets lost a little when I'm with you."

He continued looking out the window. "I don't want that," he said.

"I don't want it, either," I said.

He turned to look at the stacks of books, the pictures and pens. "I think if we lived in the same place, or if you didn't live in the same city as her," he said. "I wish I could feel differently."

I thought of telling him about how I'd felt as I kissed the barista, how he had been there with me, but I didn't know how to explain, where to even start. "You give me something else," I said instead.

And the wave again, the wish to lie down, to give. I clenched my own bones, using the pain to ground myself back in reality.

He didn't seem to hear me. "I'm sorry I hurt you," he said, looking tired and worried. "Are you okay?"

Finally, I let go of my wrist. I'd been holding on to it the whole time. "I'm okay," I said. Then, my voice a little strange to me, I added, "You don't have to treat me like an egg."

His attention sharpened. "What are you saying?"

"I can feel you holding back," I said. "With me. You don't have to."

A shadow flashed behind his eyes, light and quick, and then he returned to his exhausted form, dulled by the drive and the jealousy.

"We'll talk about it later," he said. "Do you want to go for a walk? I think I need the air."

We got dressed and left my apartment. My wrist didn't tingle anymore, but I kept reaching for it, like I wanted it to, the new feeling still dully knocking around in my chest. And so I was distracted and failed to notice that I'd led us right past the coffee shop.

"I just need to grab a coffee," he said.

"No." And as soon as the word was out of my mouth, he knew. I saw the shadow pass again, his look changing as something pulled inside of him.

Jaw tight, he turned from me, walking straight into the store.

I stayed on the sidewalk, staring at my reflection in the tinted glass, wavy and slightly distorted. The big dark windows that let you look out but not in. She could see me. I was caught, seen. And I felt an ugly, twisted thrill, a drive that pushed me out of myself until I followed him through the door.

The choreographer stood at the counter, asking the barista if she had oat milk, ordering the shop's most expensive beans. And then he stopped. He felt me, knew that I had followed. He turned to look. A surprise, and then a narrowing.

"Darling," he said, holding out his arm, "come here."

The barista's open, easy face looked at mine.

My body fell into his grip like a trained animal, letting him wrap me close.

"What do you want?" he said, turning to me. I felt his gaze, the heat of his breath.

I looked at her. "Just a coffee," my new voice said. "Room for cream."

"Your usual?" she said.

I nodded. The choreographer held me so tight his bones dug into mine. I watched as he handed across his credit card.

"Thank you," I said to her, taking the cup. I didn't meet her eyes.

We walked out together like that, as if my side had been zipped to him. Something had gone wrong with my muscles, my internal force and pressure abandoning me. Later, he'd say he had just been curious, but something changed when he felt me follow. A new line between us, opening.

"How was that?" he asked, mouth pressed against my forehead, my hair.

"You were awful." My voice sounded strange to me. Hungry.

"But you came to me," he said, his voice low and thin. "Little Rabbit. You followed. You obeyed."

"Yes," I said.

"Because you liked it."

I pushed my face into his neck, mouth open as if I could swallow him. "Yes."

His excitement breathed, a bright and sparking energy.

"What do you want?" he asked, and I didn't care that we were in public. I pressed my mouth against his ear.

"I want you to take me."

We forgot the walk, went back to my apartment and abandoned the coffee on the counter.

He didn't have to ask. "I'll tell you if something's not okay," I said.

"I'm going to be rough with you," he said. "Is that okay?"

"Yes."

He pushed me down onto my knees, his fingers pressing against my cheek.

"Just yes?"

I took one finger into my mouth, tasting salt. "Please," I said around it.

He lifted me up and put me on the bed. I reached for the button of my jeans, but he said, "No. Don't do that."

He pulled the clothes off me, unpeeling, until I was naked while he loomed fully clothed above me. "Now you can undress me," he said, and I shook as I unbuttoned, unzipped, I wanted it so bad.

"What are you going to do?" I asked, and he grabbed my face with one hand, a vise around my jaw. *He could crush me*, I thought again, my body fired, electric.

"Don't speak unless I ask you," he said. His voice sounded rough now, full and different.

He let go of my head, pushing me so I landed flat on my back, splayed open. "I might hurt you," he said in his old voice. "Is that okay?"

I felt both so empty and so full, hollowed out and ready to burst. I couldn't take it anymore, this separateness, this waiting. "Please."

He grabbed my upper arms and squeezed so I felt the vessels bleed and bloom, and then he bore down on me with his weight, thrusting in without warning. *Please*, I thought but remembered not to speak. I felt like I was cracking, breaking into him.

He grabbed my face again, making me look at him. "Whose are you?" he asked in his new voice, the question alone bringing me to the edge. "Who do you belong to?"

"Yours," I said. My voice was a whisper, but the word ripped through like a scream. "I belong to you. I'm yours."

★ ★ ★

AFTERWARD, HE WRAPPED me up in my blanket and carried me to the couch so he could watch me as he made tea. I felt empty in his arms, slack as he set me on the cushions.

He brought the hot mugs over to the couch. Brushing my hair with his fingers, he kissed my forehead, my neck. "Rabbit," he said, the name coaxing me back. "Are you okay?"

I didn't say anything. I hugged my own arms, feeling the bruises, my body strange and new.

His thumb stroked my jaw, my neck. "Was that the first time you've ever done anything like that?"

Still waiting for speech to return, I nodded.

"Did you like it?"

The words seemed to swim their way to me through the air. The trees had begun to shed their leaves, so when I looked out the window I had a small view of downtown Boston. My voice, when I finally spoke, sounded like it came from there, far away across the river. "Yes," I said. "I liked it."

"You don't make that sound good," he said.

"I don't know. Is it good?" I let the blanket drop from my shoulders, my bruises showing. He pressed his mouth to them, brushing with his fingertips.

"Just because you like it, doesn't mean it's real," he said.

I looked at my feet sticking out from under the blanket. My hands, my wrists.

"It feels real," I said.

I looked at my things, my table, my chair. The world I'd left the moment I followed through the café door.

It felt more real than anything.

CHAPTER EIGHT

I found myself on the other side of his restraint, and the answer meant more sessions of submission. My body narrowed down to a single, hungry animal, my only purpose to listen, to give. He pushed my face into the pillow, pinned my arms against the mattress, and the harder and rougher he fucked me, the more I wanted him to break me and dissolve the edges that kept me individual.

One day, he took his belt and looped it tight around my wrists, holding the knot of leather and flesh high above my head. He fucked me into my own body, alive and there and taking him in, and also fucked me out of my body until I was pure experience, just the ache and pleasure of rough loving. Surrendering, the words left me, no *bed* or *belt* or *cock*.

As I melted further into the fucking, I felt an echo of another time, the closest I'd ever come to God, on my back in a pew in a Philadelphia Quaker meetinghouse. My family had gone on New Year's Day to see the James Turrell skylight. The roof lifted to reveal a rectangle of raw sky cut into the smooth, vaulting surface. I focused so intensely on that point of light and air that my own boundaries lost meaning, turning into atmosphere.

That's what it felt like, to have his body breaking into mine. Like seeing God, like moving into light.

THE NEXT TIME I went to the coffee shop with Annie, the barista frowned as she took my credit card. "Your boyfriend's not here to pay for you today?" she said, sticking the plastic into her machine.

I heated, Annie standing just behind me. "No," I said. "He's not."

I took my coffee, my receipt, burying myself at a back table as Annie placed her own order.

"What was that?" Annie asked, catching up with me. "I thought the date went well?"

I hadn't told Annie about what had happened, the brief spectacle in front of the barista that I still didn't understand. Annie and I lived in language, but I had no words for where I'd gone, all body and pain and want.

"Yeah," I said, "but it's over."

"Why?" she asked.

Because the barista obviously would not want me anymore, but I didn't know how to explain. "He can't do it," I settled for instead. "He's too jealous."

Annie shifted farther back into her chair, her fingers wrapped around her mug. "That doesn't seem fair," she said.

"What?" I said. "What do you mean? I told him about the date and it hurt him. He changed his mind."

She looked away, down at the table. She had the expression she used when she was about to tear into a piece of writing.

"But he told you to ask her out," she said. "He should have to deal with the consequences."

Our shared understanding splintered between us, the chasm growing. "It hurts him," I repeated. "I don't want to hurt him."

She brought the mug up with both hands, sipping. "But he agreed. He knew the terms going in," Annie said. "His pain is his. It shouldn't be your problem."

I hugged myself, squeezing my upper arms with my fingers. "That's not really how it works."

She put the mug down. "You're going to lecture me on polyamory?"

"No." But I didn't have the words to span our new distance, the right bridge to bring her across. And I didn't know if she would even take it. The thought of her possible refusal cut into me, a sharp pain just under my ribs.

Annie looked directly at me now, leaving behind her tear-apart gaze for one more coaxing. "I just don't like seeing you give up something you want," she said.

The gentle brush of her attention had the wrong effect. I tightened, a wall rising inside of me. "I'm not," I said. And the surprise and force of those two words wiped the softness out of her expression.

"I didn't know that," she said. "Never mind, I guess."

She made a show of removing her belongings: her laptop, an outline, a stack of printed pages. Her things spread across the tabletop, edging me out. I watched her set up her index cards, her little scaffoldings. The right words would come to me, I thought, if I looked at her long enough. Phrases I could throw across to her like ropes guiding her along an ascent. But nothing came. I was left with my notebooks, my mess.

I fell into a rhythm of revising, cutting and circling and writing out. Focused, I sipped coffee and pushed my sleeve up to my elbow.

"What's that?" Annie stared at the dark bruise on my forearm. Before I could pull the sleeve back down, she grabbed my wrist and yanked it to her so my bare arm stretched between us. Her nail traced the discolored edges. "What the hell happened?"

"Nothing." I wanted to pull back my wrist, but couldn't, my arm losing all its agency.

"Don't do that," she said. "You don't keep things from me."

I didn't say anything, transfixed now by the waves and depths of my own markings. Like clouds, like loose particles, my vulnerability clear and clean.

"He did that to you?" said Annie.

I yanked back my wrist, pulled down my sleeve. "It's all consensual," I said. "I agreed to it."

"Whose idea was this?" she said. "Was it his?"

"Does it matter?" I said. Better than *I don't know*. Or worse. That maybe it was mine.

Her face turned soft, wounded. "You haven't told me anything about this," she said.

I leaned back. "I don't always tell you everything."

I looked at Annie and felt nineteen. That was the problem with seeing someone every day. You lose track of the changes, the passage of time.

I let my wrist go. I hadn't realized I was holding on to it again. She reached across to take my hand back, her palms around me insistent but soft.

"I'm here to talk about it if you want," she said.

I slipped my hand out. "I appreciate it," I said. I picked up my coffee. "I really do."

The chasm grew and darkened, the atmosphere turning wrong. I pretended to edit while she got to work on her outline. Her eyes kept tilting up at me, testing the air between us. But I didn't look back. If I did, I might see how far I'd gone, or Annie might catch me and force me to see. To face the person I was becoming, lost outside the lines.

THE YEAR WENT on. The great dark of winter swallowed up the day.

Snow fell outside of the Berkshires house, the pond slick with a thin layer of frosted ice. I watched through the bedroom window, lying on my stomach as fresh bruises emerged on my bare back and hips. I remembered that hot summer day, the ice room at the museum. Somehow, I'd found my way inside.

I could hear the choreographer in the kitchen, getting dinner ready. "What is this, on the table?" he said. I'd left some writing out, the odd lyric essay about eating alone. "Is this new?"

"Don't read it," I said, my jaw smooshed on the pillow. He always tried to read my things. "It's not working."

"The language is lovely." He came into the room, holding the pages. "Why do you think it's not working?"

"Annie says so." I'd finally given her something, a bit of writing to reestablish our baseline. She'd ripped in with her usual vigor.

He sat on the edge of the bed. "You give Annie everything you write?" he said.

"Since I was nineteen."

He put the pages on the nightstand, stroking my hair with his free hand. "Maybe you need a fresh perspective."

He kissed my ear, my neck. "Are you okay, darling?" he asked. "How are you feeling?"

"Fine," I said.

I turned my head to the other side, away from him. He continued to touch my hair, my shoulders.

"I'm working on a new solo," he told me. "I'm using Jackie, remember her?"

"No," I said. "You fucked her out of me."

He took my calf in his palm. "Don't say that," he said. "That's not the point."

"But it's true," I said, turning back to him. "Or it feels true. It feels real."

I couldn't keep up with all the new rooms we found in me, the things I wanted. I needed more, to tell me why my body desired.

I rolled over onto my back and pushed myself upright, leaning against the wooden headboard. "Sometimes," I said, touching my throat, "I want you to put something around my neck, like a collar, or a leash. I want to be like an animal that you lead around."

He pulled close, touching the same spot on me. "I've never done that," he said. "We'd have to get something special. I don't want to cause any real damage."

The seriousness of his attention broke me. *Ugly, ugly*, I thought, and then I was crying, pummeled by waves of shame. *What's wrong with me?* I pressed my hands hard against my face as if I could push the feelings back in.

He held me, fingers gripping my shoulders. "What's wrong?" he said. "Please, Rabbit. Talk."

"That name's not right," I said. "It's not . . ."

I choked, face hot. I must have been turning red.

He pulled me against his fully clothed body, letting me wet the fine, soft material. "You're okay," he told me, stroking my bare back. His hot breath stirred my hair. "It's been too much. We went too far, too fast. We'll slow down."

"No," I said. I sucked back the fear, the shame. I tucked it somewhere deep. "That isn't what I want."

"But Rabbit—"

I kissed him, taking his face in my hands and pressing it to my own like I could use it to stuff the crying down. He pulled back, but I kept reaching, wrapping my body around his until I felt him start to respond. Taking his hand, I placed it between my legs. His arm grew stiff, tense.

"Is this what you want?" he asked.

I closed my eyes, focusing on the pleasure as his hand softened, began to slide.

"Does this make you feel better?"

I nodded, feeling him work me until my muscles started to beat and relax, stretching open the tight, empty feeling.

I pulled him up and over me, unbuckling his belt, his pants, replacing his hand inside, though he returned his fingers there to keep working the outside. "I love this," he said, looking down at me. He sounded choked, like he couldn't get enough air. "I love you. So much."

His other hand went to my neck and found the place I wanted leashed, gripping it very lightly. No pressure, never, the air passing freely, but I sensed with thrill my proximity to real damage, how he held and controlled something crucial to my living.

"That's why you're going to move."

"No," I said, but at the same time I clenched his shoulder, pulling my bare skin against his sweater. The fabric itched, scratched.

"Yes," he said. "You'll move, and then I'll give you what you want." His hand stayed there on my throat, soft against me. "I'm going to give you everything."

I ATE DINNER naked, wrapped in a blanket. That was the game for the weekend, that I'd be naked as long as we were in the house. *I want you available*, he'd said, driving into me as sparks of want screwed under my ribs. *Vulnerable.* But I was also freezing.

Quiet, he watched me eat. "I didn't think about how cold it would be," he said. "You should get dressed."

"I'm fine," I said, cutting into my tempeh.

He stood. "I'll turn up the heat."

"No," I said, the word stopping him with its force. He looked at me, sat back down.

"Then we'll have a fire tonight."

I didn't say anything, taking another bite.

After a moment, he got up again, went into the other room and returned with a brown shopping bag. "I got you something," he said. "For your birthday next week." He left it by my chair, returning to his seat.

I would be thirty-one. Tucking the blanket under my elbows, I picked up the bag and set it on my lap. I pulled out book after book, stacking them next to my plate. He'd apparently bought everything ever written by Anne Carson.

"You were reading *Glass, Irony and God*," he said. "In Maine."

He'd even bought *Nox*. "Good memory," I said. "Thank you." I'd never seen *Float*, several thin pamphlets tucked in a plastic box.

"I liked you even then," he said, watching me. "When we were there. You were so stern. Full of purpose."

I put the books back in the bag and tried to remember what I'd been like then. How confused I would be by the person I was now. "I didn't like you at all."

"I know," he said. "I was really nervous and annoying."

I laughed. "I didn't know then that you could be nervous."

"Well, you know now."

I ate a little more. Maybe tempeh was okay.

"We should talk about the holidays."

"Already?" I said. It was only mid-October.

"I thought we could take a trip. Like to Berlin."

"What's in Berlin?"

He frowned. "Berlin."

"Oh." What was tempeh? Was it beans? "I don't really have the money." I'd already sunk so much into the train.

"I'd pay."

I stopped moving my fork and knife, staring at the food. "No," I said. "It makes me uncomfortable."

He breathed in that full-dancer way, taking in volumes of air while his torso stayed the same. "Okay."

"And I said I would spend Thanksgiving with Annie," I said, "with her parents on the Cape. And then I have to go back to Philly."

"Philadelphia," he said. "Your parents."

"Right."

"I'm guessing they don't know about your fifty-one-year-old boyfriend."

I'd never heard him use that word. "No, not . . . no."

I listened to the sound of his knife, cutting straight through the tempeh and scraping the plate. "And your parents?"

"They're dead," he said.

"Oh . . . oh, I knew that," I said. "I'm so sorry."

"It's okay."

"And your sister?" I said, just to show that I knew things.

"She's decided not to come back from Indonesia."

I would be leaving him alone. I pulled the blanket up over my shoulders.

"Your parents," he said again. "Do they know about your other relationships?"

"Yeah," I said. My mother had, humiliatingly, thrown me a coming-out party before I'd even asked a girl on a date. "They're open-minded. But also . . . intense."

"Good combination," he said. "Well, can you do New Year's, then? In New York? You don't really have an excuse. You'll have to pass through, anyway."

"When you put it like that," I said. He smiled. I breathed. "I'd love to."

CHAPTER NINE

On Wednesday, I grew older. I added another year.
After work, we all met up at the German bar, the weekday emptiness replaced with my friends. "Happy birthday, birthday girl!" Annie shouted at me, snapping a sparkly green paper hat on my head.

"Thirty-one!" said Esme.

"It's awful," I said. "Why is it so much worse than thirty?"

The bartender pushed one of the dark licorice shots at me. "On the house, birthday girl," she said.

"No, no," I said. "I have to work tomorrow." But I still took the drink, I took all the drinks, I drank them down.

"I think the thirties look great on you," Esme said, tipsy, her head on my shoulder.

"Don't they?" said Annie. "They glow."

"That's not the thirties," I said. "That's hyaluronic acid."

"Or maybe it's your *lover*," Esme said.

"Gross, Ez," I said. "Don't say that word."

"Yeah," Annie said. "Seriously."

Esme turned serious. "But that's what he is, right?" she said. "You're not leaving town just for the conversation."

I looked at Annie. She met my gaze for a moment before turning away. "No," I said. "I'm not."

Annie continued to face the bar, though I could see the edge of her frown. "Okay, everyone," she said. "It's that time."

"No," I said, hiding my face. "God no, please."

"Time for the—"

And everyone joined in.

"Birthday questions!"

"Where did these even come from?" I said. "Why do we even do this?"

Annie led the charge.

"From birthday to birthday!" chanted everyone at the bar.

"What's one thing you did this year that you've never done before?" Annie asked.

Everyone looked at me. I felt the choreographer's hands on my arms, my neck, his force crushing me.

"Published a book," I said.

"From birthday to birthday!"

"What's one thing you did this year that you never want to do again?"

I saw the barista's face. Jackie standing by the water.

"Have my press fail as soon as I publish a book," I said.

"From birthday to birthday!"

"In the next year, what's one thing you're planning to do?"

I want to be like an animal you lead around.

Who do you belong to?

Rabbit.

"Spending more time with all of you," I said.

I held up my shot glass, and everyone picked up their drinks. We toasted and I knocked the liquor back, feeling it burn on the way down.

Esme and Annie hugged me, flanking my sides. "Love you so much," Annie said.

"So much," repeated Esme.

"I love you guys, too," I said, resting my head on Esme's shoulder.

The time galloped away, and I felt light and easy. I'd call out of work. I'd give up, just once, on waking up at five A.M.

And then the choreographer texted me. *Happy birthday, my love*, he wrote. *Call if you get the chance.*

We stayed until closing, a mistake, probably, a great indulgence.

Leaving the bar, Annie and I walked together back up the hill. "What do you want to do this weekend?" she asked, looping her arm through mine.

"I'm going out of town," I said.

Her arm tightened. "But it's your birthday weekend," she said.

"Is it?"

She gripped her hands together, her arms forming a solid loop. "We always spend our birthdays together," she said.

"I know—we're together now," I said. "My birthday ended an hour ago."

"But I thought we could go for a bike ride," she said. "In the Southwest Corridor. Or we could go to the ICA."

"Why don't we go tomorrow night?" I said. "After work. It's pay what you can."

Her arm around mine felt hard like iron. "Okay," she said.

When we got back to the apartment, she went straight to her room and shut the door.

"Annie?" I said, but nothing. She had left a chocolate cupcake in the middle of the butcherblock counter, pinned by a single blue candle. I plucked it out and sucked the frosting off the end before sticking the baked good back in its white paper box.

After brushing my teeth, I called the choreographer. "Is it too late?" I asked.

"No," he said. "Not for you."

I closed my eyes and laid back on the bed.

"Did you have a good birthday?"

"I did," I said, touching my neck.

"And are you excited to see me this weekend?"

Yours. I belong to you.

"Yes," I said. "I am."

A COUPLE OF weeks later, I took the bus to Allston to go thrifting with Esme. We didn't get much one-on-one time now, not since the choreographer, since she'd moved across the city to Jamaica Plain.

"I think I need to move back to Camberville," she said as we drifted through the racks of musty clothing. Deer heads leered down at us, silver necklaces hanging from their pronged antlers.

"You should," I told her, flicking through a row of flannel shirts.

"But rent is *bananas*," she said. "Even Medford. But the Orange Line is killing my soul."

She picked up a sleeveless yellow dress with a full skirt. "Oo, you need to try this on," she said, shoving the dress at me. "It's perfect for you."

I held up the hanger. Small purple flowers covered the pale fabric. "I don't know," I said. "It's a little girlie."

"You love the femme thing," Esme said. "Don't let Annie get to you."

She pushed me toward the curtained changing rooms in the back. I closed the red velvet drapes, pulled off my coat, my pants, and sweater, then stepped into the dress, threading the cloth-covered buttons back over my chest. Esme's eye had been spot-on. The dress fit tight and suited me.

The bruises, though. Two on my left arm, one on my right. Dark red, almost like burns, the one on my forearm a ghost of his finger.

I dug out my phone and swiped to the camera app. Touching my left shoulder, I showed off the bruise. In the image, I'm biting my lip. I look young, frightened.

I opened up a text message and sent the picture to the choreographer.

What do you think? I typed.

He wrote back. *Pretty.*

"You okay in there?" Esme called.

More texts. *Buy it. Bring it to me.*

"Ez," I said. "Can you come in here?"

"Something wrong?"

"I need some help."

She stuck her head through the curtains. I saw her eyes go to the bruises. She didn't look surprised.

"Annie told you," I said.

She stepped into the dressing room with me. "Yeah, she did."

"I like it." I couldn't swallow. "What's wrong with me?"

She took my shoulders. "Nothing."

I saw what he'd do to me in the dress. He'd rip it, the buttons flying. "How could I like it?" I said. "How could I want him to do this to me?"

"Shhhh." She hugged me. She had on the same celebrity perfume she'd worn since college. Dessert-y, like cake. "It's okay. Really."

Somehow, I got out of the dress and back into my clothes. We went down the street for Korean food. Grilled eel, scallion-kimchee pancakes, hot tofu soup.

"Is Annie totally freaked out?" I asked.

"This isn't about Annie," said Esme.

"So she is freaked out."

She pointed her metal chopsticks at me. "Not the point."

I held my own chopsticks, using them to pinch some pickled daikon. "I don't really know how to talk about it," I said. Was it the pain? The pain didn't seem like the point. I didn't even feel it, not in the moment. The crush turned to pure intensity, the hurt trying to break me, to crack my container and set me loose.

Esme picked up a scallion pancake triangle, dipping the tip in a shallow bowl of thin sauce. "Remember Miranda?" she said.

I nodded. Esme's debonair butch ex. She'd moved to Seattle, but they were still friends.

"We loved this stuff," Esme said. "Intense shit. And it was great, because I trusted her."

I sipped my soup. Too hot, scalding the top of my mouth.

"Do you trust him?"

I dropped my spoon, the skin of my mouth starting to blister.

"I know he'd stop, if I told him to," I said. He'd made it clear to me after the first time. *If you don't like it, tell me*, he'd said on my couch, kissing my arms. *Rabbit. It's whatever you want.*

I looked around the restaurant, checking the empty table beside us.

"How could I want a man to hurt me?" I said, the words soft but dangerous as they left my mouth. "Why do I want him to tell me what to do?"

Esme's face stayed soft and receptive. "Would you feel different if you were doing this with a woman?"

"Yes," I said. "But it's not just—" I looked at my food. All the money, his age and power. His beauty and glamour, shining through.

He'd told me he'd stop if I didn't like it. But I liked it. I kept liking it, a long line of pleasure with no clear end.

"I can't stop," I told Esme. The more I took the more I hungered, bright and desperate. "Am I weak?"

"What? No," said Esme. "You? Never."

I could feel my phone buzzing in my pocket. More from him. I knew without looking.

We finished eating. We got our free end-of-dinner yogurt drinks, hugged, and left each other for the night.

I boarded the bus, taking a seat in the back with the paper shopping bag on my lap. As we started to move, I peeked inside. Purple flowers, yellow silk. Thin fabric, ready to be torn like tissue.

CHAPTER TEN

Though I'd known Annie more or less forever, the depths of her family money continued to surprise me. Many things I knew, of course: the Cape house, right on the ocean, her father's job as a surgeon. But new things sometimes appeared. For example, her sweet but logistically challenged mother still pulled spare houses out of her back pocket, evidence of an expansive, intergenerational inheritance.

"I loved the France house so much," Annie's mother said at Thanksgiving dinner. "We had the most splendid pool. These special blue tiles that we got in Portugal. Do you remember them, Annie?"

"No," Annie said, spearing a green bean. "I was a kid. Why would I remember tiles?"

"Annie loved swimming in that pool," her mother continued. "But we sold it, eventually. Annie hated France."

"It was always more Dad's thing," said Annie.

"That sounds amazing," I said. I'd never been to France. My parents were weird about travel, about money, despite both being university professors. ("*A public university!*" my mother would scream.)

Annie's father stood up, his phone buzzing. "I have to take this," he said. "Woman's on the table. Be back soon." He stepped out of the room. Annie's mom got up to start clearing the dishes.

"We should wait until Dad gets back," Annie said, "so he can help."

"Who knows how long he'll take?" her mother said. "Really, it's fine."

Before Annie could say anything else, I stood up and started stacking plates. "I'll help," I said, grabbing what I could and following her mother into the kitchen.

Annie's mother, it turned out, was a fan of the choreographer's. "We saw a performance the last time we were in New York," she said, rinsing off the dishes in the deep farmhouse sink. "Marvelous. It's just—you know, it's work you just feel in your body."

"I'll tell him that," I said, slotting the dishes into the machine. "He'll be pleased."

"Maybe you should invite him out here sometime."

"That's just what we need," Annie said, carrying in the left-over turkey. She went back out to grab more abandoned food.

"Don't mind her," Annie's mother said. "You know how she gets about you."

After cleaning up, I slipped into the guest bedroom to call the choreographer. The windows looked out onto the sea, the glass French doors leading to a private balcony.

"Did you enjoy your tofu?" I said.

"I did." He was visiting friends on Long Island.

I pinched the fraying threads around a hole in my sock. "Annie's mother loves your work," I said. "She said she feels it in her body."

"That's lovely," he said. "Thank her for me."

I heard a child screaming in the background, high-pitched and sustained. "Are there kids there?"

"Yes," he said. "My friends have kids."

I couldn't see him in a room with children. "I guess I should let you get back."

"I have a minute," he said. "We went to the beach. It was cold, but lovely."

"I'm at the ocean, too," I said. Strange to think of all that water, somehow part of the same form.

"Maybe we could take a trip this summer, to somewhere on the coast."

Still about the trips. "My family always takes a big trip to Monhegan," I said. "My parents have been going since they got married."

"I've heard it's beautiful."

"It is." Whatever I thought I might say hit a rock cliff, dropped in a sheer, awful plunge.

Another child screamed. I imagined warm light, dirty plates, a kitchen that needed to be tidied.

"I should let you go," I repeated. "Happy Thanksgiving."

ANNIE CAME IN as I read in bed, a brief respite from her family dynamics. "Can I get in?" she asked.

"Of course."

She lifted the covers and crept underneath, curling toward me with her hands clutched close to her face. We settled into the echo of all the other times we'd shared a bed, a tent, our soft, vulnerable bodies comfortable beside each other. "I hate how my dad never helps with the chores."

"I know," I said.

"It's like he thinks he's above it."

"I don't think he thinks that way," I said. "But I know how you feel."

She closed her eyes. "Thanks. You always do."

Annie went quiet, her breath so steady I knew she'd fallen asleep.

When I was in college, my mother asked me why I didn't date Annie. I always joked that Annie didn't seem interested. But once, I'd felt a door almost swing open. We'd just graduated, we'd gone to a bar to drink our uncertainties down. A pair of men flirted with us, but also didn't flirt with us. "Are you lovers?" one asked. "You seem like you're in love."

And Annie wrapped an arm around my waist, her head against my shoulder. "We're definitely in love," she said, going soft against me. I'd felt the opportunity form, gin-soaked and nebulous. I could do it, I knew. I could step into a life with her, something familiar with structure and clarity. But then I'd never be able to step out. I'd be within her lines forever, a shadow to her light.

In bed, Annie was not as asleep as I thought. She turned flat on her back, groaning. "Do you want to go to Provincetown?" she asked, opening her eyes. "We could go to a gay bar."

"No thanks," I said, flipping a page. "I'm kind of tired."

She rolled onto her back. "Okay," she said, looking at the ceiling. "I guess you're not really gay anymore, anyway."

The choreographer could have smashed me into the ground, he could have broken all my bones, and I wouldn't have felt so annihilated.

"What the fuck does that mean?" I said, throat tight.

She sat up. "I'm just joking."

"No, you're not," I said. "What the fuck do you mean, I'm not gay anymore?"

She sat up and flipped her golden hair onto her back. "I mean, you can identify inwardly as queer," she said, "but now you're straight-passing. You have straight privilege."

"And nothing that came before matters?" I said.

"Of course, it does," she said. "But how you're perceived matters a lot."

I felt myself shrinking from the edges of my body, gutted and ready to collapse. "I don't know why you're saying this," I said. "I think you're being cruel."

Her smooth face turned soft. She put her head on my shoulder. "I'm sorry," she said. "I'm not trying to hurt you. You know I love you, no matter what."

I stared at my knees, my feet, the toenails bare and chipped. I felt abandoned, enclosed, like Annie had leaned forward and fogged a glass divider with her breath. I'd thought we'd been traveling on one path, and now, I realized I'd been on my own the whole time.

I let my head fall against hers. "I love you, too," I said.

I HATED DRIVING to New York, and since I planned to join the choreographer right after Christmas, I took the train all the way to Philly, to Thirtieth Street Station. Passing through the grand art deco hall, I felt childhood envelope me, breathing in the smell of marble and piss and microwaved pizzas.

My parents stood in short-term parking next to their green Subaru Forester. "Welcome home, honey," my mom said, hugging me, followed by my father.

"Hey-o, Stink," he said.

They drove back up the highway to Mount Airy, where my childhood home remained much the same except for the recent addition of a KRASNER FOR DA yard sign. My parents had been intentional about filling their house with physical evidence of their lives. Plants and prints and photographs, baby pictures, the framed photo of my mother and I at the Women's March in DC. A broadside of one of my mother's poems hung above the stairs, and the bookshelves stood stuffed with proof of their separate disciplines: sociology and language poetry. Walking into the sameness felt like comfort, like breadth and safety.

"Your brother and Nora had to run to CVS," said my mom. "Oh shit—shoot." She sometimes forgot that she could now swear in front of me. "I should have told them to stop by the co-op. I need some things for dinner."

"I can grab them, Mel," my dad said. "Just give me a list."

I went upstairs to grab a shower, changing in my childhood bedroom, which, on the occasion of my birth, my parents had painted a cool slate gray. Since I'd graduated from college, they'd cleaned out much of the room and put in my father's exercise bike, but they left some signs of my existence: my high school soccer jersey, my college diploma, a photobooth strip of me and Annie and Esme.

I checked my bruises in the long closet mirror. Some of them healed, some fresh. I shivered with memory as I touched them, then covered up with a black sweater.

Downstairs in the kitchen, my brother had returned, helping my mother with dinner prep. "Stink!" he said, putting his knife down to give me a big, garlicky hug.

"How can I help?" I asked, grabbing a cutting board.

"Honey, you just had a long trip," my mother said, cracking the sternum of a chicken.

"The ride was easy. I just slept and read."

"That's the nice thing about trains, huh?" she said, snapping the hip joints. "I wish the government would make them more accessible."

"Only rich people take the train," my brother said. I thought about all the money I'd spent that year. "You'd be, like, using taxes to help executives."

"That's exactly what your father always says," my mom said.

"Well, Dad's right."

"Don't say that," said my mother, wielding a large meat cleaver. "Don't say to me, 'Dad's right.'"

"What am I right about?" My father walked through the back door, arms full of reusable bags.

My mother turned to the cutting board, blade down. "We're talking about trains."

He put the groceries on the counter and hugged my mother from behind. "About how government support would be a subsidy for the middle and upper middle classes?"

My mother looked up as if asking the universe for help. Really, though, it was to lean her head into my father so he could squeeze his cheek into her temple, a soft hand on her upper arm. Then he let her go and went to set up the snacks.

I found a knife and dug the leeks out of the shopping bag, slicing them at a station next to my brother.

"How's Annie?" my mother asked as she slid the chicken and fingerling potatoes into the oven.

"She's good," I said. "You know, conquering the world."

"That a girl," said my mom.

"Hey," my brother said, "what happened to your arm?" Without thinking, I'd pushed my sleeves up to my elbows again.

"I ran into something," I said, pulling the sweater back down. "A tree, I think."

"Let me see," my mother said, washing the chicken off her hands. Still wet, she grabbed my wrist and pulled up the fabric. "Oh, ouch, hon. Do you want some arnica?"

I yanked my arm away. "No, I'm really fine." And that was more or less that.

The next day, we went in shifts to Uncle Bobbie's, the local bookstore, to pick up last-minute Christmas presents. Our parents went in the morning, while Neil and I went in the afternoon.

The choreographer called while I was at the far end of the store from my brother, my arms full of gifts. "Hey," I answered softly. The people reading on the couches looked up and glared.

"Are you in a library or something?"

"Bookstore. Christmas presents." Patti Smith for my dad, Saidiya Hartman for my mom. My brother and Nora had been more of a mystery, so I'd picked a book about modern bread-baking.

"Lovely." Looking at the books in my arms, I realized I hadn't thought of anything for the choreographer. I started cruising the shelves again, desperate.

"What are you getting me?" I asked. "There's no more Anne Carson."

"I'll think of something," he said. "In the meantime, I'm ordering supplies for New Year's. What do you want to drink?"

"Whatever?"

"I'm telling you that you can pick."

I ended up in poetry. A huge white book: *The Gorgeous Nothings* by Emily Dickinson. We'd gone to her house together over the summer, taken a tour with a man who smelled like cat piss, and stared at her small white dress.

"Gin, maybe," I said. I leaned the volume against the shelf, flipping one-handed through the photographs of envelopes, poems written in penciled cursive. The pictures stood out against the white background, vivid and alive. "Or bourbon."

"I'll get both."

I tucked the book under the rest of my stack, hugging them to me. Neil had already checked out and was waiting for me in the café area. "I should go," I said.

"Alright," he said. "Love you."

"What?" But he'd already hung up.

ON CHRISTMAS MORNING, my parents made pancakes and bacon, chopping and mixing and standing side by side in the kitchen. As a child, they'd looked like twin walls standing over us, protective, until one day Neil and I caught up with them in height.

We walked the food off in the cold, muddy Wissahickon before settling into Boggle and gift-giving. I drank too much eggnog, wondered if vegan eggnog was a thing.

"Tomorrow, we're not cooking, we're not cleaning," my mother announced, pushing the latest load into the dishwasher. "We're going into the city."

"I have to stop by campus," my dad said, drying a pot. "Housekeeping. So I might not join. Is that okay?"

"As long as Neil drives." Driving in the city made my mother anxious.

We ate lunch the next day at a new Indonesian place in South Philly, the narrow streets crowded with hordes of day-drinking Santas. I felt very warm and stuffed, so eased by my lunch beer that I didn't have my guard up when we ran straight into Jackie.

"Oh my fucking God," she screamed, her arms wrapped around me. I froze, my family watching from behind me. She was with two other women, and they were all dressed as reindeer, battery-powered lights glowing through their plush antlers. "I can't believe it's you."

"Hi, Jackie," I said, pulling my shoulders up toward my ears.

She released me from the hug but held on to my wrist, her eyes swimming with drunkenness. "These are my cousins," she said, pointing to the other reindeer-women. "This is my boss's girlfriend or wife or whatever."

I felt my mother stiffen.

"Oh, shit." Jackie covered her mouth. "He's not here with you, is he?" She was truly wasted.

"No," I said. My voice sounded quiet, far away. "He's still in New York."

"Excuse me," my mother said, pushing forward to stand in front of Jackie. "Who are you?"

Jackie finally let go of me. She looked at my mother, smiling. In the gray sunlight, I saw that she was in fact around my age, maybe older, although she continued to pitch her voice young. Loose with alcohol, she'd lost some of her poise, her open control. "I'm a dancer," she said. "I dance in her boyfriend's company."

My mother's smooth appearance returned, tucking the information away. "Nice to meet you," she said.

"I can't believe you're here," Jackie said to me. "I really need to talk to you. How long are you going to be in town?"

"I'm leaving soon," I said.

"I'll meet you anywhere. Really, I need your help."

"If it's with him, I can't help you," I said. "I don't interfere."

"It's not him, it's you," she said, taking out her phone.

I gave her my number, if only so she'd let me go, then trundled off with my family, all of us silent until we got back into the car.

"So you're dating someone new," my mother said. I'd taken shotgun, so she sat behind Neil with Nora.

"Yes," I said.

"And you didn't tell us," she said. "Why not?"

"He's older," I said.

My mother leaned forward in the seat. "How old?"

I inhaled deeply, filling with air. "Fifty-one."

She propelled herself backward, hitting the seat with force. "Oh, honey," she said, "are you sure?"

"Yes," I said, staring at the highway. "He's also an Aquarius."

"That's . . . wow, that's old," said Neil.

I watched through the side mirror as my mother turned left, looking out her window. "Is it serious?"

I turned to the right. I could feel the choreographer's hand on my neck. *I love you.* "It might be," I said.

She wrapped her arms tight under her ribs. "Well, let's wait a moment, maybe," she said, "before we tell your father."

SHE TOLD MY dad right away, of course. I knew because I could hear him on the other side of the house, shouting, "WHAT?"

Jackie texted me that night asking to meet the following day. I suggested a bar in my parents' neighborhood, hoping the trek would throw her off, but she still took a rideshare all the way out to Mount Airy.

I watched her enter the bar, dressed again in her trendy insufficient jacket. She slid across the booth from me, just a wisp in the vinyl seat. She didn't look at all the way she did onstage, commanding and full of power. Here, she looked nervous, checking her reflection in the bar mirror. Another small woman. Annie would make some joke about her, I thought. Annie would try to feed her soup.

The waitress came and took our orders, brought our drinks. We held the cold glasses like stage play props.

"Thanks for showing up," Jackie said. "Nice meeting your family yesterday."

I said something inconsequential, sipping my beer. I was angry, even though it wasn't fair of me to blame her.

"I really do need your help," she said. She picked up a paper coaster and started ripping the layers with her long, polished nails. "He's been very unhappy with how I've been dancing."

"Like I said—I don't intervene," I said. "I don't see how I can help you."

She looked away from me, gripping her drink.

"I know," she said. "I'm losing it a little, I think. I'm desperate."

"Apparently," I said. "If you're coming to me." I remembered how the choreographer had said he wanted the dancers to be more like me, failing to measure the distance between our disciplines.

"I'm just not used to something like this," Jackie said. "He's never told me to do this before. *Refer.*"

"What are you talking about?" I asked.

Her hands began to fly in front of her, as if she had to move in order to think or speak.

"We don't point to anything," she said, "when we dance. We're don't reflect the world in any specific way. We just do what we're doing."

I felt my brain slip, her words just beyond my understanding. "Then I really don't see how I can help you," I repeated. I thought of myself as a reference machine, absorbing and pointing and representing. Like Annie, who thought our writing ought to reflect and say something clear about the world. Sometimes, though, I worried about this, that I might only be good for imitation.

"But this part is different," she told. "The part is you."

A raging itch swirled on the surface of my skin. I started to scratch my neck, my elbows. "I don't understand."

"Neither do I," she said. "That's why I wanted to talk to you."

The itch turned into a choke. Jackie didn't seem to notice. She kept talking, as if the woman across from her had not been changed to hot stone.

"What does he tell you to do?" I asked. "Is it inspired by me? What does he say?"

"No," she said. "He says the solo's you. Not for you, but you."

I looked at my hands on the sticky table. Small. Trapped and useless.

"He's always been an 'intellectual,'" she said, air-quoting. "I'm used to that. But what am I supposed to do with this?" She made a throwing gesture, like she'd found something disgusting. "Something abstract but also so specific."

I looked at my wrists, my arms on the table across from hers. Unmuscled and vulnerable, still bearing marks.

"What do you want from me?" I asked.

"I don't know," she said. "I guess—what is it about you? That he likes? What would he want to use?"

Her question juddered inside of me, setting off sparks. I could move again. I stood up. "I'm not telling you that," I said. I got out some bills for the beer, throwing the money on the table.

"What?"

"I'm not telling you about us," I said, pulling my arms through my coat. Easier than saying that I didn't know the answer. "I'm sorry, you're on your own."

I turned away, I left, disappearing through the door as she screamed, "But my ride cost *forty dollars*!"

I called the choreographer as I walked back to my parents' place, feet tripping on the uneven sidewalk. "I just had drinks with Jackie," I said. "Remember her?"

"Yes?"

"The dancer you once pretended to fuck me like, who's now doing your solo? Your solo that's apparently me?"

I could hear myself breathing through the phone, rough static.

"She told you that." I imagined him pinching the bridge of his nose, what he must be doing with his hands.

"She wanted help," I said. "She asked what you'd like to take from me and put into a dance."

He laughed, a choked, horrible sound. "She asked you that?"

"What's the answer?" I said. I was crying now, ugly, frustrated tears. "What are you doing to me?"

"I'm not doing anything to you."

"Then why the solo?"

"Because I love you," he said. His voice rose now, beginning to unravel. "I love you, and so you come into my work. Doesn't that make sense to you?"

"You're trapping me."

"No," he said. "I only do what you want. Do you love me? Do you care about me at all?"

"Of course," I said. I almost slipped on ice. I'd come to the front of my parents' house without realizing it. "Of course I do," I repeated, as if that were enough.

He breathed against the surface of his phone. When he spoke next, his voice had returned to his control. "I'm sorry I didn't tell you," he said. "We'll talk about it when you get here."

The warm light spilled out from the front windows, illuminating me.

"No," I said. "I'm not coming."

I hung up, shut off the phone, following the stairs back inside.

CHAPTER ELEVEN

I found my mother sitting on the floor of her office surrounded by several sheets of white computer paper. Each page had a single word printed on it in giant sans serif font. She appeared to be working with only prepositions: *of, at, to.*

"Is Dad around?" I asked.

"No," she said. "He's off doing something essentially masculine with your brother."

"Oh," I said. I'd always found it slightly easier to talk to my father.

"Is something up?"

I reached back to rub the tight ridge of shoulder muscle. "I might stick around for New Year's," I said. "Is that okay?"

She looked up. She knew. She always knew. It was why it was hard to talk to her.

"Of course," she said. "We're going to meet friends for dinner in West Philly—do you want to join?"

"No, I'll just hang out with Neil and Nora."

The force of my mother held me in the room. "Sit down," she told me. "By the 'to.'"

I sat, a cross-legged mirror of my mother. The older I got, the more my body revealed itself as an echo of hers.

"I'm sorry that yesterday I reacted so . . . strongly. To your . . . your news," she said. "I didn't mean to. I want you to know I trust your judgement."

"Thanks, Mom."

She looked down at the splay of words. "I know I can't keep you from being hurt, honey," she said. "I just don't want you to be used."

I pulled my knees up, hugging them close like a child, with my toe still stuck under the *to*.

"Mom, do you ever write about Dad in your poetry?" I asked.

"All the time." She laughed.

"Does he mind?"

"Completely," she said. "But he knew what he was signing up for."

She shifted the placement of *with*. I wondered if Jackie's revelation would have made me so uncomfortable if the choreographer had imprinted me in words instead of another woman's body. The squares on the hardwood floor looked safe, contained.

"Anyway," my mother said, putting the *with* back, "it's not like my work makes a lot of sense."

BACK IN MY room, I switched on my phone. The choreographer's call came through.

"We need to talk," he said.

"I know," I said.

"Please don't end this."

I stared at the ceiling, the pattern of nested fans drawn into the once wet plaster. "I'm not," I said. "I just need a little space."

I SPENT NEW Year's Eve in Center City with Neil and Nora and a cluster of high school friends, listening to a drunken countdown as a tray of hot dogs turned beside me. At the bar's version of midnight, I watched my brother kiss his wife and thought of the choreographer. *What if he kisses someone else?* I let the idea blossom into ache.

When we got home, I checked my phone. Annie had texted a cartoon version of herself riding a unicorn, *Happy New Year!* surrounding her as bubble letters. I sent back a cartoon version of myself with the same application, though mine rode a dolphin.

Nothing from the choreographer. I'd told him not to. What had I expected?

The next morning, I got up and packed my bags. My parents were alone in the kitchen. My mother sat at the table trying to livestream the Mummers' Day Parade on her laptop while my father putzed around mixing himself yogurt and muesli.

"I thought we weren't supposed to watch this anymore," my father said, standing behind her and looking over her shoulder. "I thought it was sexist or racist or something."

"There's supposed to be a queer troupe this year," my mother said, leaning forward and tilting the screen.

My father put his hand on my mother's shoulder, and I watched, neither one aware of me, as my mother reached up and wove two of her fingers into his.

I walked into the kitchen, my parents shifting. "Hi," I said. "I'm ready to go to the train."

Rabbit, his email began.

I know you need some space, and I'll give it to you even though it hurts. But I need to tell you the moment I knew I wanted you. You probably think it was your night of daring, when you jumped into the lake, but it wasn't. It came before.

I noticed you right away of course, but then there was an incident you probably don't even remember. You were walking past my studio. You were always walking past my studio, and the crunch of your footsteps was beginning to annoy me.

But one day the crunching stopped. I looked out the window, and you were crouched down on the path. You were looking at something on the ground, something too small for me to see. But I could see the intensity with which you studied it, like you could dissolve yourself through fine attention. And I realized, there she is. You've found her.

I didn't respond.

I remembered what it was, of course. It was a beetle, alien and fat.

DURING MY LUNCH break, I went out for a walk just to feel my body, even as the bitter wind cut through the warmth and puff of my down coat. The river had frozen over, a thin white sheet breaking as it met the rocks and dead weeds by the shoreline.

I stood on the bridge looking down at the ice and imagined dropping a stone so big that it would break through. I imagined myself a stone so big that I would break through.

I imagined the choreographer's love as a fall into the frozen river, losing myself in the dark water like a soft annihilation. What would happen when I needed to surface and found the hole frozen back over.

What he did, I wanted, true. And I feared what I wanted, the urge to jump over, dive deep. What he'd done was crack something new inside of me and let it break the world.

In the morning, I wrote the choreographer alive so I could see him on the page, made him solid to study what he'd done to me. But it wasn't quite right. From life to page he'd gotten twisted, I'd twisted him, so he wasn't really the same.

I made one half of the writing the choreographer, one half a young dancer who might be a stand-in for me. Written down, the choreographer turned cruel, manipulative, taking hold of the woman who was as blank as the pages I hadn't yet filled. He narrowed her world to just her body, then made her body his, forcing her to spin and lift and fall.

The work possessed me, seized me, until I was no longer a woman writing but writing taking the form of a woman in order to be born. I sank down, surrendered, waiting for the words to teach me about my life. But the choreographer wasn't the choreographer. Written, the choreographer was me, and the dancer was me, too, and I made him hurt and punish her for all the things I wanted him to do to me. Because I still wanted him to do things to me. I wanted to rest at his feet and put my face against his knee. I wanted to look up into his face and tell him I was his.

At the end of the writing, I thought I'd discover something new about the two of us. But he wasn't there at all. All I'd found was myself, alone in a closed room.

★　★　★

"I THINK IT's definitely weird," Annie said. "Why would he make a dance thing about you?"

We sat cross-legged on colorful mats covered with thin yoga towels for soaking up our sweat. Annie, sensing my vulnerability, had finally convinced me to go to hot yoga.

Coils glowed above us as vents pumped hot air into the room. Class hadn't begun yet, but the windows were already steamed with heat, my water bottle covered in its own condensation. I dabbed my dripping neck and face with one of the studio's starchy towel rolls. *I'm not going to get through this.*

"He says it's because he loves me," I said, drinking from my water bottle.

Annie looked at the last of the ghostly bruises on my bare, sweating arms. "I think there are other ways to show love."

I retied my hair tight against my scalp as sweat oozed between the follicles. I wished I didn't have any hair. The heat made me wish I didn't have any skin.

"So you don't think I should stay," I said.

Annie didn't look at me. She wiped her own neck and chest. "I think you should do what you want," she said.

More people kept coming into the room, each addition bumping the temperature up by another few degrees.

"But if you're around more, we could go to the Cape house, like we used to," she said. "We could do another mini writing retreat this weekend."

"That would be nice," I said.

We had to squish together and stagger our mats so we wouldn't graze each other as we rose and turned and lunged. The men wore tight shorts, no shirts, hairs sprouting along their shoulders. The women stripped down to sports bras, sweat pearling on their bare necks, the middle of their backs. I took another drink of water, horrified that half the bottle was already gone.

I looked at the bodies in the room, all of us turning into puddles on our individual mats. *We're so alone inside ourselves*, I thought. Bumbling through the world, trapped. But with him, I'd felt my body go gaseous, expand. I lost myself in the world we made together, dissolving into shared oblivion. As emptiness, I had found myself no longer so alone.

The teacher entered, shutting the frosted-glass door to seal us in our sweat and heat. "Welcome, everyone, to your heated seventy-five-minute power flow," she said. "It's going to get pretty toasty in here, but we ask that you stay in the room." Somehow, her skin stayed powdery and dry. "So grab your water bottles and remember to keep breathing! This is your time."

We got on all fours. I couldn't believe I'd paid twenty dollars for this.

She ordered us from forward fold to plank to downward dog, *chaturanga*, and crescent moon. Sweat poured from parts of my body I hadn't even been aware of. The air became so damp and thick with everyone's breath that my skin felt slicked with collective perspiration.

The heat opened my veins as wide as tree trunks so my heart had to pound to keep up with the new volume. Every time I stood and lifted my head, I felt the blood pour down too quickly, spinning the world. *I'm not going to make it through this.*

"Is everyone feeling the heat?"

My flesh hit its melting point, my covalent bonds loosening. I would die if I stayed here any longer.

I stumbled across the studio, trying to avoid people's arms and legs as droplets of sweat flicked from their fingers and toes. Then I had the door handle, pulling it open and launching myself into the relative cool of the studio lobby. I felt immediate relief, landing on the ground with the wall at my back in a nest of muddy boots crusted with sidewalk salt. My body began to solidify again, my veins shrinking as my heart returned to a normal rate.

The front desk girl brought me water in a little paper cone, a fresh towel for my red jelly-face. "First time?" she asked.

"Yeah," I said. Even the inside of my throat felt like it was sweating.

"It's super intense," she said, but she hugged herself, shivering with performed pleasure. "But afterward, you feel so good."

Then she went back to her place by the computer, leaving me close to heatstroke on the ground.

BEFORE WE WENT to the Cape, we did our laundry in the building's ancient machines, dragging heavy bags up and down from the basement. Sitting together on the couch, we folded, sharing a bowl even though weed tended to slow the process down.

"That's pretty," Annie said. She watched me fold the yellow dress, the one with purple flowers.

"I bought it with Esme," I said. I checked the buttons, their threading. They'd held up in the wash.

I'd brought the dress to him in the snowy mountains. "Put it on," he'd said. "No underwear." I pulled off my clothes, my sweater, my jeans, giving in to the pleasure of his orders.

The choreographer sat on a kitchen chair, watching as I pulled the dress up over my shoulders, my fingers shaking as I threaded the buttons. But he didn't make me come to him the way he usually did. Instead, he got up and caught my elbows, pinning me against the edge of the table with his hips.

His right hand gripped just under my jaw. He wouldn't touch my neck again, not even when I asked. Danger, risk. But he got close enough to raise my heartbeat, forcing my face up to his.

"Do you want it?" he asked, his other hand reaching under the hem to trace my bare hip. I tried to say yes, but I'd been stripped, reduced, struggling to nod against the vise of his fingers. "Then you have to be good."

He kissed me and then lifted me, slamming my body onto the table and ripping the dress the way I knew he would, the buttons popping off like loose teeth. I lay open, exposed, crying as his mouth brushed and bit my soft flesh.

I don't remember how he became undressed. I must have undressed him, must have obeyed his instructions to take off his clothes. But I left on my broken outfit as he strapped up my arms and fucked me hard into the solid wood.

But after, he knelt and gathered up all the buttons, picking them out from under the cabinets and between the floorboards. "Let me fix it," he said. He'd sewn himself into a hundred delicate costumes, had done the same for other dancers.

I took the dress off and handed it to him, wrapping myself in one of his loose rehearsal sweatshirts.

"Won't you just tear it again?" I asked, watching him with the sewing kit. The needle slipped through his nimble fingers.

"Yes," he said, not looking at me, "but then I'll fix it again."

He finished the work, the buttons back to new.

Now, Annie watched me looking at the dress, but she didn't see what it held for me. "I like it," she said, "even if it's kind of girlie."

* ★ *

THE NEXT DAY, we loaded Annie's car with wine and weed and chocolate chip cookie dough, a whole chicken to roast, and boxed baby lettuce. Then we threaded the car through the tunnels of Boston to make our way to the Cape.

"They're giving me the spring conference to organize this year," Annie said as we crossed the narrow Sagamore bridge.

"That's great, Annie," I said. "You've been wanting more responsibility forever." The conference stood out as the literary nonprofit's crown jewel, a multiday event drawing the writing stars, the agents, and editors. Donations and registration fees fed the nonprofit all year.

"I can't do anything drastic with the lineup, but one day, I'm going to make it my own," she said.

"I'm sure you will."

She leaned on the gas, the Volvo speeding through traffic. I closed my eyes, listening to the sea-soaked wind. I loved going to the Cape with Annie. Fast lanes, open doors, the world unspooling before us.

As we neared the ocean, the highway narrowed to a two-lane road buffered with scrubby pine trees. In college, we'd throw parties at the Cape house, skinny-dipping in the freezing sea. Now we went with our coolers full of groceries, pretending to be well-to-do, sedate.

The choreographer didn't pretend. He just was. I felt the beat of missing him, then tucked it away. Not this weekend.

We had the snowy beach to ourselves, walking along in our down coats as we passed the open wine bottle by the neck. High sand dunes rose on one side, held up by roots and sharp saw grass. I spotted a wishing stone, picked it up as though to give it to the choreographer, then threw it over my left shoulder even though I didn't know what to ask for.

We climbed an old wooden lifeguard stand, abandoned for the season, maybe for good. I stumbled, one-handed with the bottle, and Annie caught me, helping me finish the climb.

"Look, there's a seal," Annie said, pointing to the water. I saw a dark, strangely human head bobbing near the break.

"So close to shore," I said.

"The fishermen hate them, but I love them," Annie said, passing the bottle back to me. I took a glug.

"When was the first time we came out here?" I asked. "Sophomore year?"

"Freshmen year. Fall break," she said. "Oh my god, we trashed the place."

"We did not *trash* it."

"You threw up in my parents' bathroom sink."

Oh yeah. "Whoops," I said. "I'm glad they still like me."

"Of course they do," Annie said, wrapping her forearm around mine. Her fingers slid up my palm, lacing through the web of my fingers.

She'd gripped my hand just like that all those years ago during our first college party on the Cape. Late at night, we'd snuck out, just the two of us, as the rest of the party began to drift and wilt. I stumbled barefoot down the dunes, Annie laughing as she guided me through the sandy brush. Drunk, happy, I laughed, too, following her down to the ocean, to the beginning of our lives.

We wrapped ourselves in one blanket and lay alone on the sand, the stars and moon shedding their cool silver light. Annie took my hand under the wool, and I squeezed back, a buzz of pleasure radiating through touch. I'd found her, my people, my person, my life dropping into gear. She'd found me, too, we'd found each other against all the odds that we'd remain apart. A miracle, to collide straight into the right person for your life.

Now, on the lifeguard stand, I held on to Annie's fingers. "Is that oyster bar in P-town open all year?" I asked.

"I think so," Annie said. "You want to go?"

"Yeah," I said. I rested my head on her shoulder. "Let's live a little."

Dollar oysters, an early sunset. Walking through the dunes at the end of Massachusetts. I felt giggly from champagne. "Just the tip," I laughed. Annie howled, the wind taking her voice.

"Gross."

"There's got to be a bar here called that," I said.

"Ugh, stop it." Her face revolted. I threw an arm around her.

"You really don't like the penile, do you?" I laughed, my mouth close to her face.

We made it back to the glowing windows of the house and got the chicken in the oven, but instead of sitting down with plates, we stood by the marble counter and picked at the tender meat like feral animals. I mulled wine with orange juice and cloves while Annie baked the cookies, and then we settled with our laptops under blankets, working. "How's it going?" Annie asked, looking at me and my laptop.

I had the dancer story open in front of me. I'd meant to put it away—working on it next to Annie made me feel oddly exposed—but I kept returning. As I moved around clauses and tested rhythms, the story filled the space around me until it had nowhere else to go but inside. Even as Annie spoke, I felt something split, an odd hum taking over my body.

"It's okay," I said.

"Do you want to watch something?" Annie said. "Something creepy."

"Oh no," I said. We'd always been at odds when it came to horror movies.

My phone buzzed. A text message. *Don't look*, I thought, but then I did.

I need to see you.

I put the phone down. But then another.

Rabbit. Please.

I put my laptop down on the marble coffee table, dropping my phone into my pocket. "I'll be right back," I said.

Back to the guest room, but it didn't feel far enough. I wrapped up in a spare blanket and slipped out onto the balcony. Below, the dark ocean roared, the roil and power of pure water.

He picked up right away. "My love," he said. I closed my eyes and gripped the wooden railing, pressing his voice against my ear. "It's time."

The wind tore my hair, cut my cheek. "Alright," I said. "Okay."

I PACKED MY bag for the weekend. Sweaters, pajamas, jeans. Then I saw the big white book, *The Gorgeous Nothings*, which I'd hauled all the way from Philadelphia. I used my hands to measure its weight and heft, then put the book inside my duffle bag and started getting ready to leave.

I'd agreed to go to the Berkshires house, but only if he'd pick me up. I thought I'd punish him with traffic. Only when he texted his ETA did I realize how stupid I'd been.

"I'll be trapped if things go bad," I told Annie, filling my water bottle in the kitchen.

"Don't worry," she said. "I'll drive out and pick you up, if you need me to."

"That'd be four hours of driving."

She crossed the space and gave me a quick hug. "I'd do it," she said. "I just want you to stand your ground."

"Okay," I said, although I didn't know what ground I was meant to stand on.

I knew he'd arrived before he'd even texted me, a slight lurch below my ribs guiding me to the window.

He could never remain in a confined space if he didn't have to. I watched him get out of the car, waiting outside in the cold. The sight of him made my chest beat, *Oh, beauty*.

"You've got this," Annie told me, squeezing my shoulders. "Call if you need."

"I will," I said. "See you later."

As I approached, I panicked, not sure how to greet him. I ended up hugging him with just one arm, jutting out my shoulder as a barrier between us. "Hi," I said, my body already going to melt, rebelling against me.

"Hello," he replied, taking my bag and putting it in the trunk.

We got in the car and started driving down the hill toward the river and the city. "How was your New Year's?" I asked.

"We don't have to do this," he said. "The small talk."

We drove down School Street, heading through Cambridge to get onto the Mass Pike. "I'm sorry," he said. "I should have talked to you about the solo."

I swallowed. Voice firm. "Yes, you should have."

The car was full of his smell, his heat, and my body started to lean toward him, moth straight to flame. *Stop*, I told myself.

"I realize it was unpleasant to hear about it from Jackie," he said. "But I don't understand, still, why you're so angry."

We passed the river, coming close to the towers. "I feel like you're taking pieces of me," I said, "and using me for work."

He shook his head. "That's not it at all," he said. "It's honor. It's love."

My chest and stomach began to feel pressed in on all sides as if their internal atmosphere were losing volume and density. "I feel like you want every part of me," I said. I thought of the agent, of Jackie. "Like you're trying to find your way inside."

"Maybe I do," he said. "Do you not feel the same?"

"No," I said. "I don't." We had different ideas of loving. He would find his way to all my desires until he'd found ones I hadn't even discovered. He'd plunder me just to please me. But I wanted him apart and golden, something distant to admire.

"I don't want to change you, or hurt you," he said. His mouth opened but then shut, more to say but no way to say it, the feelings trapped and turning pressurized inside of him.

My throat began to thicken and close. "I just never thought I would be this," I said. "Someone's little woman."

"Is that what you think?" he said. "I don't see you that way at all."

I saw Annie, the agent, even the barista, his hand reaching out to pay. "It's how others see us."

"Fuck others," he said. He swore so rarely, it gave the word more punch.

We crossed the bridge and stopped at a light. I saw myself at the door of his house, playing the smiling hostess.

"It's how I see us," I said.

He did the dancer-breath again, and I waited for him to speak.

"I wish I could change that," he said.

The light turned green. He didn't move fast enough. *HONK*. "Green," I told him.

At the next light, the last before the highway, he reached into the backseat and tossed a small cardboard box into my lap. "I got you this," he said. "For the holidays."

I pulled apart the paper edges, unfolding to reveal pale pink silk. Lifting the ribbon from the box, I saw that it was some kind of tie made from loops and thread, delicate and strong.

"It's specially made," he said. "So it won't pinch or choke."

I wrapped the ribbon tight around my fingers, binding them, then brought the fabric up to my nose. Floral, powdery. The pulse again, radiating from my chest to the distal ends of me. Why did I want this so bad, this chosen fright.

"Are you going to put this on me?" I said.

The question rippled through him, his jaw muscles flickering. "Is that what you want?"

I let the tie go so it turned loose and harmless in my lap. My veins had opened up again, heavy with fresh blood. "Yes."

He gripped the wheel, staring hard at the road. "Okay."

By the time we got to the house, the sun had begun to set over the tree line. "I had to turn off the water," he said. "So it'll be a second."

I brought in my bag, leaving it on the floor next to the bedroom as he disappeared into the basement. I could see my breath in the air, the heat on just enough to keep the pipes from freezing. Raising the thermostat, I turned on a few lights and took off my coat, still shivering. On the table were things I'd picked up during hikes: pinecones, feathers, rocks shot through with green.

"Rabbit."

He stood on the other side of the room, fingers combing back his hair. He looked at me like I was unexpected, something precious that he'd found.

He came to me quickly, his force lifting me and taking me to the bedroom. My body sighed as it touched his, long-held tension suddenly released. My hands in his hair, mouth on mouth, on skin. "I missed you," I said, his touch pulling the words out of my throat. He moaned nonsense into my neck. *Darling* and *love* and *dear*.

Clothes gone, sloughed off as if by magic. Our bare skin shrank in the cold, but we didn't notice, sustained by our own heat. I'd been ready since the pink tie, the car, and so I pulled him into me.

His hands gripped my upper arms until I felt the inner tendons shifting, his weight pushing me into the soft bed. My neck arced and I gasped, looking up at him. All the things I wanted done to me, a new one flashing through. "Will you hit me?" I asked.

He stopped. "What?"

"My face."

"No." He let me go, backed off, turning limp. "No, I don't like that."

I sat up. I felt the urge, the curiosity, as well as the dampened ache of shame. "You hurt me all the time."

He shook his head. "I'm rough with you during," he said. "But I don't want to hurt you just because. I don't like it."

"I don't understand," I said, crawling on all fours toward him.

He touched my arm, tracing a nearly invisible bruise. "This," he said. "It's about letting go. Being with you. I—"

His voice stopped, stuck, his face above me both frightened and tender.

"It's not about hurting you," he said.

"Have you tried?"

"Rabbit." But I nuzzled my face against his thighs, taking him whole in my mouth the way I knew he liked. "Rabbit," he said again, but his voice sounded full of extra air, his hand on the side of my neck.

I gripped the rest of him in my hand and worked the length until I felt him at the edge. Then I stopped and looked up at him. "I won't finish until you hit me."

His mouth tightened, a *no* just under his expression. But then he threw me on my back, the force surprising me, and slapped my head to the side. He'd kept his hand open, the force light, but still his fingers stung across my right cheek.

I turned back to him immediately. His face screwed with pain, then hollowed out, empty.

Pushing off the bed, he went to the other room and sat on the wide, cushioned footrest. He seemed to deflate, curled over his torso in a rare moment of bad posture.

I got up and followed. "I'm sorry." I'd gone too far. I'd fucked up. "I'm so sorry."

"I don't like that," he said. "Don't make me do that again."

"I'm so sorry." I dropped onto the other side of the footrest, pressing my hurt face against his back to let the stinging cool along the knobs of his spine. "I fucked up."

"This isn't about punishing you." He twisted around to face me. "Is that what you want? To be punished?"

I remembered the story sitting on my laptop. "Yes. No. I don't know." I felt the choke again, a fresh heat spreading across my face. "I don't know what's happening to me. I feel very . . . I'm lost." I breathed in the smell of him, his scent not like anything else.

My face was wet. I was crying without realizing it. He wiped at the tears, then scooped me up. "Come here," he said, pulling me onto his lap. "Be sweet."

I rested my head on his shoulder, turning toward his neck. I felt so tired. "I really missed you," I said. I'd never get away from it.

His fingers found my chin, tugging it up so he could kiss the line of my jaw, my cheek.

"My family knows about you," I said as his mouth moved lower.

"Mm," he hummed against my throat.

"They don't like it."

"Not overly surprised." His lips brushed across the stem of my neck, the skin lighting up as he traced.

"Do you ever get shit for this?" I kept speaking, but my body was already responding, pulled into him. "For us."

"No," he said. He moved down to my chest. His hands. His mouth. "I think the expectations for men like me are much lower."

"I get shit for this."

"I know." I gasped, spine bending, all stretched out now on the footrest as he shifted his body above me. "Sometimes I think it's selfish of me, to keep you."

I'd reached the edge, the precipice. I looked down, let go.

"Keep me," I said. "I want you."

He took me slow and gentle there in the living room, plumbing for my most tender parts, so that when I finally came I broke into crying, a fumbled, shattered relief. "I love you," I told him, and, exhausted from want, we stayed wrapped in each other on the floor.

Chapter Twelve

He didn't get me back to Somerville until late Sunday. Annie stood in the kitchen, mixing soup. "Hello, Annie," he said, following me through the door. She looked up, registering his presence.

"Hi," she said. Then to me, "I didn't realize we'd be having company."

"Last minute change," I said. I found the parking pass on the mail table and handed it to him. "I'll handle the bags," I said. "Go put this on your dashboard before you get a ticket."

I put the bags in my bedroom and came back out into the common area. "Is he staying for dinner?" Annie asked me.

"He's staying the night."

She looked at the apartment door. "How is he going to get back in?"

"He has a key," I said. "I gave him one."

She turned back to the soup. "You should have asked me."

"I know," I said. "I'm sorry."

She raised her elbow as if mixing thick cement.

"We'll go out for dinner," I said.

"No, it's fine," she said. "There's enough soup for us all. It's vegan, too."

I stepped behind her, hugging. "It's like you knew," I said. "Thanks."

We sat at the table and ate the lentil soup, Annie and the choreographer squared off at either end while I occupied the middle.

"How's your work going?" Annie asked the choreographer. "I hear a lot about your dances."

The choreographer blew on a hot spoonful. "It's going well," he said. "I mean, it's hard to talk about."

"I bet," Annie said.

I added some salt to my bowl.

"And you?" he said. "I hear you work in fundraising?"

"Yes," Annie said. She spoke at some length about the literary nonprofit. "We hold classes. We create community."

She turned to me. "We should talk about the conference," she said. "We're inviting some really great people. Lots of agents. Let me know if you want me to set up a consultation. I can get you a discount."

I swallowed my food. "Annie," I said, wiping my mouth with one of her cloth napkins. "I have an agent, remember?"

Sometimes I thought I was the only one who held the key to her face. The little flares of her nostrils, the lines that tightened around her eyes. "Right," she said, turning back to her soup. "I forgot. You haven't talked much about her."

"I haven't sent her anything yet," I said. "I'm still working on stuff."

"Like what?" Annie said.

"Like that food essay."

"I thought that wasn't working," she said.

I met the choreographer's eye. "I'm just getting a fresh perspective," I said.

Alone, curled up in bed, the choreographer whispered, "I don't think she likes me very much."

I kissed him lightly, holding his head with both hands. "She's just protective."

"You need protecting?" he asked, his hand sliding up my shirt.

"Yes," I said. "Extremely."

I turned off my five A.M. alarm but still woke up before him. His lovely smooshed face. His long limbs bursting out of my bed. He woke as I got dressed for work. "That's what you wear to the office?" he asked.

"Yep," I said, adjusting the edges of my gray tweed skirt.

"You don't look like you at all."

"You don't see me during the week," I said. "Monday through Friday I'm the office drudge, remember?"

"Mm. Strange."

He got out of bed, rubbing his face awake as he stood over my desk. "What's this?" he said, looking at the marked-up story draft.

"That's nothing," I said, reaching over and grabbing the pages. I flipped them facedown and shoved them into my desk drawer. "Something that's not working out."

He brushed his teeth and shaved in the bathroom. I met Annie in the kitchen, both of us in our polyester work clothes.

"Did you have a nice night?" she said.

"Yes," I said. I looked in the fridge for something vegan. Fruit? "We didn't disturb you?"

"No," she said, pouring coffee into the travel mug she latched on to her bike. "I wore my headphones."

The choreographer stepped out of the bathroom. "Morning, Annie," he said. She made a grumpy dog noise in reply.

"I don't think I have anything you can eat," I told him.

"You could always go to the coffee shop," Annie said.

We looked at each other, the choreographer and I, holding the gaze for a little too long. "There's a Portuguese diner down the hill," I said. "Let's go there."

"Sounds great," he said. "I'll grab my bag."

"Have a nice time," Annie said, watching us go.

The weather was chilly and gray. "She definitely doesn't like me," he said as we walked down the sloping sidewalk.

"She takes some time to warm up," I said.

"And if she never does?" he asked.

"She will," I said. "I didn't like you at first, either."

He took my gloved hand, kissing the fabric fingers. "I had a slightly different agenda with you."

After breakfast, he dropped me off at work, parking illegally in the lot across from the law school quad. "So this is where the magic happens," he said, putting on his blinkers and getting out of the car.

"Hurry up," I said. "You're going to get a ticket."

He came around and kissed me, cupping my face with both hands. "It's worth it," he said.

Some new force pulled me toward him, a fresh heat pulsing through my chest. "I don't want you to go."

"If you moved, I wouldn't have to."

"Not now," I said. "One thing at a time."

"Okay." I kissed him, my hands clinging to the front of his coat. I wanted to seal my body to his through all our layers, stretching the contact out.

"I love you," I said.

"You've said that quite a lot," he said, holding on to my elbows.

"I'm practicing."

He kissed me again, even though I was late, he was late. He needed to make afternoon rehearsal. "I'll see you next weekend," he said.

I stood outside as the professors and students passed, watching him get in the car and drive away.

I ENDED UP staying a little late at work. Annie was home by the time I returned. She'd ditched the work clothes, sitting in sweats at the table with her laptop.

"Please warn me the next time we have guests," Annie said. "I didn't have any soup for lunch."

"I'm sorry, Annie," I said, taking off my shoes and stretching out on the couch. "I'll make dinner tonight."

I pushed up my sleeves out of habit. She looked at my new marks. A bruise on the forearm, a friction burn on my right wrist. But nothing on my neck. The tie didn't leave anything behind.

"So everything's alright with him?" Annie said.

"Yes," I said, still staring at the ceiling. "Everything's back on track."

Chapter Thirteen

When I put on the pink tie, I became a different animal, his animal, my whole body intent on what he wanted, on finding my own desires. The more I gave, the more I sank into a heady love, my body emitting strange vibrations. I'd look into his face sometimes, take it with both hands, astonished. *How did I get here?* I wondered. *You are so unexpected.*

IN LATE JANUARY, my friend from graduate school, Ian, emailed asking if I wanted to join his reading series in Queens as an event for my book. I'd forgotten that I'd talked to him about it, back when my book had felt like the beginning of something. *Sure,* I emailed back, letting him add me to the lineup.

"Where is it?" asked the choreographer over the phone.

"Ridgewood."

"Which trains go there?"

"Do you not go to Queens?" I said.

"Don't do this, Rabbit," he said. "Don't make me feel old."

I sucked back the next biting thing on my tongue. I hadn't done this yet, brought him into a part of my world.

I left work early, getting onto the train with a Rollaboard suitcase filled with copies of my book. Somewhere around Stamford, I changed in the bathroom, breathing in pee and hand sanitizer vapors. Black jeans, my dark velvet top with the keyhole choker neckline, my silver earrings that pointed down like daggers. Bracing my elbow on my knee to counteract the jolting, I leaned close to the buffed metal mirror and applied my makeup mask, heavy eyeliner and dark shadow smudged to smoke.

I went straight from Penn Station to the bookstore, agonizing over the start and stop of the subway as the time clicked closer to late. Finally, I emerged, getting to the corner and finding the choreographer waiting for me on the frozen sidewalk.

He saw my face, his expression turning to strange wariness. "You look different," he said.

"Do I?" I jittered with prereading nerves. Performing was not why any of us wrote. I didn't want to remind people of the fact of me, to put my face on the line and invite exposure and comment. I'd rather stay in the background, listening and absorbing.

Ian's voice called out my name from the doorway of the bookstore, his familiar short frame blocking the entrance. I hadn't seen him in a moment, but he looked the same. One of my betas, he wore his lank blond hair overgrown around his ears. "You fucking stranger," he said to me. "I heard a rumor you're here every fucking weekend."

"Not quite," I said, hugging him. I introduced the choreographer. "My partner," I said. "He lives here."

Ian took in the choreographer's gloriousness, shaking his hand. "You're the one keeping her from us," he said.

"I wouldn't say that," the choreographer said. "She has free range. And she wouldn't be here if it wasn't for me."

Ian hunched up his shoulders, then turned to me as he pulled a metal flask from his jacket pocket. "You got the jitters?" he said, holding it out. "It's your favorite."

"Thank you," I said, accepting the flask and taking a big gulp.

The bookstore's café area had been cleared to make space, the display tables rolled into the back. My books went on a four-top repurposed for merchandise, posed alongside the records of an avant-garde sound poet.

The choreographer did look wrong in the room, not because of his age but because of his clean beauty. Seeing his spine among the rest of us felt startling, a contrast to the normal person's hunch.

All the coated bodies turned the small space warm, and I started sweating under my arms. "Alright, everyone, take your seats!" Ian shouted at the milling crowd. "Reading's about to start."

I had a text from Annie. *Go get them bb!*

Ty! I typed back before swiping the phone to Do Not Disturb and sticking it in my bag.

Taking a seat near the front, I clenched the choreographer's hand. Despite the warming glow from Ian's flask, the jitters got bigger and louder.

Ian had stacked the event with five readers in order to draw a crowd. I waited, listening but unable to absorb. When my turn came, Ian introduced me as his friend from graduate school with her book from the "now defunct Three Lemurs Press." I let go of the choreographer and stepped onto the makeshift stage.

Odd how a piece of writing can quickly turn into an artifact. Holding the thin paper covers of my book, I felt like I'd unearthed something hidden below layers of a new self, a fossil preserved in sediment.

Flipping to the dogeared page, I found the passage I'd picked on the train, then leaned close to the shitty microphone Ian had stolen from his band. I lost track of my feet, my hands. *Don't read like a boring writer*, I reminded myself. *Slow*, and then I began, dissolving into the words.

When did the crack in the road appear? No one really knew. It probably started out as a sliver, nothing to be noticed, peeking open a hair more as each car jolted above it. And the jolts grew harder as the crack grew bigger, the hard cement beginning to soften and warp.

They closed the road too late, of course. It had already done its damage. Further repairs needed, they claimed, but no repairs would ever be made.

On a bright, fall day, the Anderson kid crossed the barrier. He smelled the sulphur, saw the rising smoke. Clouds of gaseous air that his senses knew were poison. But the poison pulled him anyway, steadily closer even as his eyes began to bleed. The crack was a chasm now, the air above it distorted, hot, and the Anderson kid walked straight into it, never to return.

That was a bad ending, I realized as I spoke. I could have found a better word than *return*. But still the applause, my friend Vera whistling from the crowd, and I finally shuffled back to my spot next to the choreographer. He kissed my ear. "Wonderful," he said.

I actually sold some books, shoving the cash into my coat pockets. Beer money. Cream-cheese wonton money. None of it felt real. Loose and heady with adrenaline, I kept taking nips from Ian's flask until I started losing track of my limbs.

The choreographer met Vera and also Rita, my friend who lived in Sunset Park. They admired him visibly, feeding my pride at having dragged this glorious air spirit into my underground lair. "Is this the guy taking up all of your time?" Rita asked, smiling at him.

"Your friends keep saying that," he said to me, his arm heavy around my shoulder. "Should I be flattered or worried?"

"Both," Vera said.

I leaned my head into him. "We went to graduate school together," I explained, gesturing at the two women. "They're hobbity gremlins, too."

"Not really. I haven't written a word since fall," Vera said. "Rita's still going, though."

"Academia doesn't count," said Rita. After our MFA, she'd gone straight into a comp lit PhD program at Columbia. "I just regurgitate what people have already said about Georges Bataille."

Someone passed with smoke in their hair, the scent sparking an old urge. "Do you have a cigarette?" I asked the choreographer.

"Of course I don't," he said.

"Ian just stepped outside," said Rita.

"Great, I'll be right back," I said, squeezing the choreographer's hand.

I stepped out into the cold, the cutting air briefly sobering. Maybe not a full one. I found Ian standing a little further down the street, smoking with a group. "Could I have a sip?" I asked, tapping his shoulder.

He smiled, shaking his pack. "No," he said, "but I'll give you your own."

I took it gratefully, then listened to Ian's plan to go to a beer hall around the corner. Apparently, they sold drinks by the boot. "What does that mean?" I asked.

"The glasses are really shaped like boots."

The choreographer walked out of the bookstore, tightening his coat around his neck. I stubbed out my cigarette and went over to him. "We're going to a bar nearby," I said. "Do you want to come?"

"No, darling," he said, both hands taking hold of my cold cheeks. "I think I'm going to head home."

Strange lines cut into his face, an unfamiliar expression. "Is everything okay?" I asked.

He let me go, looking over my shoulder at the cluster I'd just left. At Ian. "Have you slept with him?" he asked.

I swallowed. *How did he know?* "Only the once," I said, "many years ago."

The pain moved as a light tightening across his brow. Now I reached out, took his head in my hands. "You have to stop this jealousy thing," I said.

"I know." He held on to my wrist.

"Are you sure you don't want to come?"

"I don't think I've read up enough," he said, pulling my hands from his face. And even in my inebriation, I saw that the problem was not his age but that somehow, impossibly, he felt inferior.

"Don't be silly."

"I'm serious. I'm tired," he said. "I'll take your bags. Stay out and have a good time."

I pulled him in by the front of his coat, stretching up to kiss him. I held the kiss even as I felt Ian watching, the heat of my friends' eyes inside the bookstore. Then I let him take my bags and watched him walk away to the train.

On the walk to the beer hall, I checked the time on my phone and saw another text from Annie. *How'd it go?* I shoved the phone back in my pocket, my gloveless hands freezing in the cold.

The beer hall had been in the area long before the neighborhood started gentrifying, and we were not exactly welcome. Still, the hostess led us past the rows of glamour shots, all the Miss Little Polands since 1962, bringing us to a table in the corner of a windowless room.

We got our beers—no one chose the boot—and listened to Ian talk about his plan to quit his job and work full-time for Bernie Sanders.

"Ian, what the hell do you know about political organizing?" I said.

"Just because my dad's not a tenured political scientist, doesn't mean I can't have views," he said.

"He's a political *sociologist*," I corrected. "And I'm not saying you don't have views. I'm saying you don't have skills."

Vera let out a low *Oooo*.

"I have plenty of skills." Ian picked up his glass, red in the face.

"As a poet," I said. "We should support people who know what they're doing."

Ian pushed his beer forward on the table. "Fine, whatever," he said. "How's writing going?"

"It's fine," I said.

"Things working out with the agent?" asked Rita.

"I don't know," I said. Each time I thought of the agent, I saw Annie's face, her lingering wisp of judgment. "I haven't really sent her anything."

"Where did you find her, anyway?" asked Vera, adjusting her lipstick line with her pinky. She'd recently switched from fiction to screenplays, hoping to make more money.

"Honestly," I said, "him," and they all knew what I meant.

"Damn," said Rita. "So that's the dance guy you came down to fuck last spring?"

"Yep," I said. I'd forgotten that I'd told her, how explicit I'd been about my plans.

"So where did you find *him*?" asked Vera.

"Yeah, seriously," added Rita.

"A residency."

"God, I need to do one of those," said Vera.

Ian listened to us going back and forth, sipping his beer. "He doesn't really seem like your type," he said.

"Absurdly good-looking is everyone's type," said Rita.

"Is he rich?" Vera asked.

"Sort of," I admitted, and Vera held up her manicured hand, waiting for a high five.

At the end of the night, I hugged everyone good-bye, reluctant to start the long subway ride back to the choreographer's. "Thanks for inviting me," I told Ian. He lived just a short walk away.

"Of course," he said, zipping up his coat. "Don't be a stranger, C."

I didn't get back to the choreographer's until very late, or more accurately, early. I drank a glass of water mixed with vitamin powder, hopeful hangover preventative, then took a quick shower to wash off the train and beer and cigarette.

Body-tired but still wired from the night, I found my slouchy sleeping clothes, my retainer, then crawled into the choreographer's bed, his breath steady and deep. Closing my eyes, I focused on the sound, letting it lull me into rest.

★　★　★

IN THE MORNING, my eyes felt gummed-up from leftover makeup, but my hangover prophylactic appeared to have worked. The sunlight pouring onto the ceiling did not cause my skull to burst.

He turned beside me, already awake, and kissed my night-stale mouth. "Go brush your teeth," he told me.

I went to the bathroom and popped out my retainer to brush and scrub myself clean. When I emerged, he stood in the living room, waiting for me with the pink tie in his hand.

"Come here," he said.

Walking slowly, I crossed the room and stopped in front of him, my hands and arms shaking.

"Good girl," he said, kissing my clean skin. "Sweet Rabbit."

He looped the tie around my neck, tucking it under my hair before sliding it tight against my skin. I kept my eyes on him the whole time, the shaking turning to seismic tremor.

"Take off your clothes," he said.

He told me to suck his cock without touching the rest of him. The task was more difficult than expected, balancing on my knees with my hands clasped tight behind my back. When he was close, he made me stop, then fucked me on all fours with the tie taut in his right hand.

After, he removed the silk gently, kissing my neck, my shoulders, and arms. Our rough fucking always left me emptied out, and so he used his mouth and fingers to retrace my edges, summoning me back inside.

"Are you okay?" he asked.

"I'm wonderful," I said, kissing his forehead. "I didn't wake you when I came in?"

"No," he said. "You were as quiet as a mouse."

We made breakfast, cashew yogurt and chia seeds for him, scrambled eggs and toast for me.

"How was the rest of the night?" he asked, pouring more coffee.

"Fun," I answered, spreading fake butter on my toast.

"Good," he said. "You looked happy. You looked right."

I piled some of the scrambled eggs onto the bread. "Why are you jealous of Ian?" I asked. "It seems a little absurd."

He poured in the oat milk, stirring. "Like I said, you looked right."

"The age thing?"

"And the brains," he added.

"That's ridiculous."

"No, it's not," he said. "To dance, you have to give up a lot."

"You have to do the same to write."

He put down the mug, his attention on me almost physical. "You don't seem like you've given up anything," he said. "You seem exactly where you belong."

I felt hot; I didn't know what to say. I stood up, reaching for cooking utensils, cups. "Here, let me help clean up."

I threw out the coffee grounds from the ceramic pour-over cone. "How's your work going?" he asked, rinsing out the enamel pan.

"It's good. It's fine."

"Anything I can read?"

I poured the last of the coffee into my own mug. "Maybe," I said, sipping. "I just need to fix a few things." I hadn't looked at the dancer story since we'd made up in the Berkshires. The draft existed somewhere between dread and thrill, its odd power lurking beyond my computer screen. I still didn't know what any of it meant, what the story had to do with me.

We finished getting dressed, then went to the Met, where I hadn't been in some time. We wandered through the regular exhibits, trying to avoid the roving families and tour groups, and were about to leave when a woman called out his first name.

She was around his age, her silvered hair pulled back in a tight chignon. Her appearance was polished, costly, and I thought that she looked like a stork, her thin neck rising out of a dark coat folded around her like a funeral lily.

He put on the face I'd seen with Franny and Dodge, the donor face, plus an additional, incremental grimace. "Cynthia," he said. "How's Harry?"

"He's fabulous." Her glance barely passed over me. This happened a lot, when we were spotted by his people.

But he didn't make a point of introducing me, and that was how I knew.

"How's the new work coming?" she asked him.

"Good. It's going well. Looking forward to showing everyone."

She kept her face turned away from mine, looking at me with only her eyes. "Who's this?" she asked.

He said my name, his voice smooth, removed. "My partner."

I felt the full breadth of our age difference then, the force of what she thought of me imprinted on my skin. *Young. Vapid. Gold digger.*

"Is your new piece about her?"

"It is," I said. She kept her preternatural, smooth face still, but I could feel her surprise at the dumb young woman, speaking. "Partly. Is that something that happens often?"

Her mouth puckered. Something sour on her tongue. "Only when he's strongly affected." The elegant stork mask returned, a light professional friendliness. "Well, we all can't wait to see it," she said.

She burrowed deeper into the Egyptian wing while we left the museum, exiting into the park. "So that was your ex-wife," I said as we wandered paths surrounded by mounds of dirty snow.

"How did you know?"

"She looked at you like she owned you."

He pulled his coat tighter, straightening the knot of his scarf. "She sort of still does, in a way."

The skin around my neck turned hot and tight. I forgot the morning, the pleasure of the night before. All I saw was the way she looked at him, the sort of look I never wanted pointed at me. "So is that what this is, then," I said. "You and me? Am I *compensatory*?"

"What are you talking about?"

My eyes burned at the corners, stung by the slight leak of angry tears. "She owned you, so now you own me."

"Oh god, no, Rabbit." He grabbed my upper arm, but I yanked it away.

"I'm sick of that name."

"Please, darling, don't be jealous—"

"Jealous?" We stopped, blocking the path. Lovers spatting by the bushes. "Is that what you think this is? I feel *dirty*."

I walked away, feet crunching on sidewalk salt. He caught up, got close, hissing in my ear.

"So maybe some of it is compensatory," he said. "Maybe I want to spend money on you, and help you, because I've been helped and spent on. What's wrong with that? Why do you hate it so much?"

My breath flared now, enraged. "My dad once wrote a book about rich people and their dogs," I said.

The non sequitur stunned him. "What?"

"He used the dogs to study their child-rearing practices. But he didn't have to get IRB approval for the dogs. And do you know what kind of dogs rich people like? The ones they keep?"

"I don't know, Pomeranians?"

"Rescues," I said. "The ones with three legs and PTSD and high vet bills. Projects to spend their money on and make them feel good about themselves."

He grabbed both my arms, pulling me close. His skin glowed with angry heat. "Don't you dare," he said. His rage shook through me. "You have no idea what it was like for me. You have a master's degree, skills. You can have a desk job, do other things, go anywhere. I went to conservatory. I can only do one thing, and I have to live here to do it."

For the first time, he wouldn't let me go, even though I wanted him to.

"No art is pure, Little Rabbit, not even yours," he said. He tugged me closer, breath on my skin. "We live with money, so get used to it."

I couldn't wait to bite back, except I got so angry I burst into tears, an unfortunate kink in my wiring. Seeing my face crumple and wet, he panicked, hugging me into his chest. "No, no, I'm angry," I said, but still I wailed like a helpless child.

His chest heaved from effort and rage, but he started smoothing my hair, kissing it. "God," he said, "how can you think I actually own you when you make me look so stupid?"

I cried harder, forced my face into his coat. At least I would stain it.

"Breathe, my love," he said.

"Don't tell me what to do," I said. But I did breathe in just the way he'd shown me once, deep belly breaths to massage and calm the nerves.

Finally quiet, I left the park with him, both of us wrapped apart from each other in our own coats. We went to a nearby restaurant for dinner, a small place with low lighting and a wall of ancient, mottled mirrors. I watched the waiter guide our reflections to the table. *Does he think that I'm his daughter?* I wondered.

At meals like this, I didn't know what to order, not sure if I would manage the fight over the bill or just give in and let him pay. I settled on chicken instead of duck, a side of arugula, and a glass of the second-cheapest white wine.

He watched me cut into the meat. "How are you feeling?" he asked.

"Not now," I said. I didn't want to cry again, something more explosive about tears indoors.

"Fine," he said. "How's the chicken?"

"Delicious." I ripped meat from bone. "The farro and squash?"

"Very good."

Everything we didn't say drifted around us, wringing us out. The waiter brought the bill and I put down my card, too. For once, the choreographer didn't fight me.

We went back to the apartment, exhausted.

I sat at the table as he uncorked the Montepulciano, fetching two glasses and pouring a generous amount in both. He settled on the other side, both of us drinking and not looking at each other.

"Honestly," I said, "I was bothered that she looked at me like I was a dumb slut."

The language physically grated him. "If it makes you feel better, she looks at me the same way," he said. "It's more or less how she looks at everyone."

I finished the last of my glass. He reached over with the bottle, pouring more. "When did you meet her?" I asked.

He topped himself off, then took the cork and stuffed it back in the bottle's neck. "I was a little younger than you," he said.

I sipped. "You must have been unspeakably beautiful."

"Not grizzled and ugly like I am now."

I pulled my bare feet up on the chair. I'd ditched the itchy sweater tights as soon as we got home. "You're still gorgeous, and you know it."

He dropped his head to the side, watching me. "You know, what we do, it's play," he said. "It's not real."

I pushed the base of my glass in a circle, swirling the red wine. "It feels real to me," I said. "In the moment. And I want it to be, when it's happening. I want to be . . . nothing. Not me." I tried to find the right expression. Words like *owned* and *object* and *thing*. But none of them worked. They didn't fully capture what I got when I gave.

Heat rose up my neck and fanned across my face, but I maintained steady eye contact.

"I know," he said. "But even then—it's still play."

Play just didn't feel like enough. Not the right word again. I felt stuck, lost. "I'm sorry about what I said. With the dogs," I replied.

He sipped. "Thank you," he said. "Although on further reflection, I guess it's somewhat accurate."

"Still. I know I'm not pure."

Putting down the glass, he looked out the window. "You know I think you're brilliant, right?" he said. I flushed. "That's also why I want to help you."

I pulled my knees closer to me. They looked knobby and young. "Thank you."

He drained his wine, staring at the empty glass. After a moment, he pushed it aside, then got on all fours and crawled to me across the floor.

"What are you doing?" I stuck my legs down, pushing my chair away, but he still caught them, kissing my bare calves and pulling my pelvis to the edge of the seat.

"How do I convince you that this is pure?" he asked, pushing up the skirt of my dress. His teeth nipped my inner thigh, a hot spark lighting me up.

"Sex doesn't solve everything," I said, but I'd already dropped my head back, my dress up above my hips. He peeled off my underwear, throwing it away.

"But you're so easy to please." I cried out, proving him right as he circled and licked and kissed.

I came still half-dressed on the chair, and then he pulled me down onto the floor with him, taking off his clothes, my bra and dress. He touched all over, gathering me up like cloth in his fist. "Rabbit," he said as his hands gripped my hair, his mouth on my forehead. "Please."

Pulling away, he looked into my face, desperate. I nodded. "Break me," I said.

He slammed my arms above my head, pinning me to the hardwood as he pushed in, his want shuddering through me. "No one gives like you." He bore down on me with his hips, his weight, his eyes staring with wonder and need. "My darling, my girl."

I shattered, I came. I broke and turned to God, to nothing, scattering in a million pieces below him.

I BOARDED THE train to Boston one bag lighter, the suitcase of books left in the choreographer's spare closet. He had space, I told myself. It wasn't like I was moving in.

I settled into my seat, taking out my laptop and finding a new email from Annie. Strange, since I would see her in less than five hours.

Hey Babe!

Hope everything went alright! You didn't text me back, but it's fine. I bet you were just busy.

Something jolted in my chest. A tightening, a warning. *No,* I said to my body's little flaring signals. *Nothing here, no threat.* All I had was an email from Annie.

I've got great news! A presenter dropped out of the conference, so I can slip you in. Just a two-hour craft talk, but you'll get free admission to the whole event. And the parties! You can do your experimental thing. It'll be great exposure for you. Lots of people to meet.

Let me know soon. It's the first weekend in April.

Big hugs and kisses,

—A

Great exposure, lots of people to meet.

I started typing in the email box.

Sorry I didn't text.

I stared at the words. I deleted them.

Yup, big weekend this weekend!

Wrong also. Delete.

Sounds good about the conference, I wrote. *Let's talk more about it when I get home.*

Xoxo, C

I hit Send.

I stared out the window, watching the ocean pass. *She just wants to help.* Hadn't Annie always wanted to help me?

But still the email stood as a weight on my chest, a limit on my breathing. *Help.* What did that mean, and where would I find it?

I started a fresh email, typing in the agent's address.

You seem exactly where you belong.

Your experimental thing.

I opened up the Word document with the dancer story. The words pulsed with heat, the sentences opening and unfurling. What I'd hit had seemed like a wall, but now I saw that the wall was really a door, and not just a door but a portal to step through and a barter to make. No art was pure, after all. Not even mine.

I went through and changed the gender of the choreographer character—I wasn't stupid—read through for spelling errors, and attached it to the email. *I'm not sure if I want to send it out,* I wrote to the agent, *but tell me what you think.*

Chapter Fourteen

I like the depiction of the couple. The relationship has a nice frisson, the agent wrote back. *I think it's ready to send out. Just give me the word.*

I read the email while the choreographer prepared drinks in the kitchen of the New York apartment. Scanning through it again, I decided to wait, closing the laptop. I had a party to get ready for. Shower, a black dress, makeup, and gold hoops. The choreographer's birthday.

As he set out the spread of nuts and bean dips, I lit candles around the apartment and turned down the lights, my reflection chasing me in the dark windows. A little woman. *Fuck you*, I thought to the shadow.

I'd been told to invite some of my own friends, a mix-up of our lives. Rita couldn't come, but Vera showed, and so, confusingly, did Ian.

"Wow," Vera said as I opened the apartment door. She wore a black-and-gold sequined dress, clutching an "Aquarius" pillar candle with a ribbon tied around it. "I really need to go to a residency."

Next to her stood Ian, bottle of red wine in hand. "Hi, Ian," I said. "What are you doing here?"

"I'm Vera's guest," he said. "You told Vera she could have a guest."

"Okay," I said. "Well, welcome. Let me take your coats."

Most of the choreographer's friends had already arrived, mingling in the slightly altered common space. "Did your darling bring fresh blood?" asked Ron, the composer. He studied Ian openly.

"She did, apparently," said the choreographer. "Hello, Vera. Ian."

"Hi," said Ian. "Happy birthday."

"Thank you," replied the choreographer. "Can I get you a drink?"

"Sure," Ian said. "Anything with gin."

I put the coats away, placed the candle and the wine with the other gifts on the counter. Vera strolled around the space, taking in the furniture, the artwork, dollar signs popping out of her eyes. Ian also looked around the apartment with a measuring expression, though his study came with a different kind of enthusiasm.

"You look like a proper housewife," he said, following me into the kitchen area.

"Fuck you," I said, spooning vegan paella into a serving dish.

The choreographer stood out of earshot, talking to Vera and Ron by the windows. "Seriously, what kind of corporate sponsorship does this guy have?" Ian asked.

"Ian, you're a UX designer," I said. "You work for an app about pet food allergens."

"So? I help people."

"Venture capital is still capital." I lifted the warm paella dish with both hands, carrying it into the party. Ian tried to follow me but got waylaid by another former male dancer who managed the choreographer's theater.

Vera pulled me aside. "Are any of the men here straight?" she asked me.

"Besides mine? I don't think so," I told her.

"Damn." She pointed at the green Icelandic dish the choreographer used to hold his keys. "I remember cataloging that when I worked at Sotheby's."

The party dizzied me with its tasks, its energy. I refreshed drinks and snacks, brought out more paella, chatted and joked and tried to bring Vera and Ian into the mix. I carried out a chocolate cake made with aquafaba and coconut whip, the blazing candle cuing everyone to sing. Then I cut little slices of the cake and handed them out to the hungry.

"Darling, drink," the choreographer said, handing me a glass filled with something amber and orange-smelling. "Relax."

"Are you happy?" I asked. "Are you having fun?"

He touched my jaw, pinched the hoop of my earring. "Yes," he said, "I am."

His friends started clinking their glasses, calling for a speech. "Absolutely not," he said.

"Give us a rough temperature check, at least," said Ron. "How was your year?"

He didn't look at anyone else in the room. He only looked at me. "I'd say it was a good one."

Before I gave out, people finally started to leave.

"Invite us over again," said Vera, standing in the hall.

"I will."

"Are you moving here?" Ian asked. "Like, here specifically." His eyes measured out the structure around us.

"I don't know yet," I said.

Ian stuck his hands in his coat, hunched up his shoulders. "Let me know," he said. "I can get you a job at the dog food app."

When I closed the door on the last guest, the tension released from my body, my shoulders dropping. "Oh god," I said, rolling my head and rubbing my tight neck. "I hope that went well."

I turned around. The choreographer stood in the center of the room, smiling at me.

"What?" I said, touching my hair.

"You just looked very comfortable," he said. "Tonight."

I remembered the summer at the Berkshires house. I didn't know, exactly, when the pretending became real.

People had cleaned a bit, but we still had a lot to do. Wineglasses to gather, little dishes of cake to find in strange locations. I blew out all the candles, filling the air with wisping smoke.

"Did you have a good time?" I asked again.

"Yes, wonderful," he said, gathering the plates that had ended up on top of his books. "Your friends fit in nicely. Ian was a big hit."

"Fantastic," I said, rinsing off a cutting board covered in cilantro leaves.

"Still don't totally understand why your ex was here, though." He filled the paella dish with rogue glasses and brought it into the kitchen.

"Once again, twelve minutes after the UMass Book Festival doesn't make him my ex," I said, taking the paella dish. "And he was Vera's guest."

The choreographer grabbed the cleaning spray and a rag. "Is he threatened by me?" he asked.

"Of course," I said. "You're extremely threatening."

The choreographer didn't reply, smiling to himself as he wiped down the table.

He left briefly to Skype with his sister in the other room, then called me over. "One last task," he said. I came in and crouched myself into view of the web camera. Even badly pixelated, I could tell how much she looked like him, dressed in white linen before a hot Indonesian morning.

"I've heard a lot about you," she said.

"Me too." I shouted at the screen as if trying to make up for all the distance. "Nice to meet you."

Dazed with post-party exhaustion, I tried to stay attentive through the brief conversation. Who I was, what I did. "A wonderful writer," the choreographer said, touching my hair, and I remembered the story on my own computer, the agent's email, and the back of my neck prickled.

"You seem smart," she said, and, with gratitude, I felt the conversation start to close. "I'm glad."

"Thanks," I replied. "Have a good morning."

He x-ed out the screen, closing the laptop. "She'd get along well with my mom," I said, standing up. Knees aching, I walked toward the door.

"Melanie Tsang?"

I stopped, turned back. "Did you Google my mom?"

"I've actually read her poetry," he said. "I think. Before I met you."

"Wow," I said, "you should tell her that. Attention and flattery are her weaknesses."

I walked back into the kitchen. I'd put it there now, between us. The imagined future day.

As I scrubbed the paella pan, my hands sudsy and wet, I felt the pink silk tie descend around my head. The pan fell back into the water, my hands still dripping.

He took his time, pulling my hair through and shortening the loop so the fabric sat flush against my skin. The kitchen, cleaning, all the menial tasks fell away as my systems came fully online.

"Kneel," he said. I lowered to my knees one leg at a time. He shifted behind me, standing close, the other end of the tie light in his hand. "Look down."

I kept my eyes where the cabinet met the tile. My breath came through my mouth in thin slips.

"Do you like this?" he asked, tugging the silk as his other hand played through my hair.

"Yes."

"What does it do to you?" he asked.

I dropped into my body, my chest, looking for the language. "I feel excited," I said. "I feel frightened."

His body burned behind me, radiating through our clothes. I couldn't wait. I struggled to keep my hands loose, my body obedient.

Then he dropped the tie. "You can get up," he said. We were done. "You should get ready for bed. We've got a big day tomorrow."

AS WE WALKED through the door of the school/practice space, we covered ground rules. "Obviously, no sex stuff," I said. "And you can tell her I'm bi or whatever, but maybe not that I'm attracted to her specifically."

"No, of course not," he said. He wouldn't look at me the whole subway ride over, his body tight and anxious even though it had been his idea. Or maybe it was mine. I couldn't remember anymore.

We walked together down the hall. I slowed. "Why her?" I asked, voice soft. "Why did you have to use her?"

"She's my favorite dancer."

"I know that's not it."

I stopped. He took a few more steps before stopping as well, turning to me without meeting my look.

"Is it because I like her?" I asked. "Is that why?"

He finally raised his eyes to mine. "Yes."

My jaw clenched, muscles ready to bite. "I'm not a joke," I said.

"Of course," he said. "That's not what I mean."

"Then why?"

"There's an energy there. I can't really explain it," he said. "But it has to be her."

Now I turned away, staring at the floor. I felt open, unprotected. Taken and totally seen.

He came close, touching my cheek, his fingers guiding my chin. "Please trust me," he said.

I stepped back, my jaw slipping out of his hands. "Fine," I said. "Okay."

Jackie waited for us in the studio, warming up. She swung her arms, drew hip circles to massage the femur head in the pelvic socket.

"You're not dancing," the choreographer told her.

"I thought we'd show—"

"No." His hand gripped the back of my neck. "She doesn't get to see it until it's done."

He pulled a chair into the middle of the room. I sat with my hands in my lap, staring at my own reflection in the big wall of mirrors as the choreographer and Jackie watched from the side.

"I'm not really sure what I'm supposed to be getting out of this," said Jackie.

"I don't know, either," I said. "It's not like I can just be myself on command."

"Rabbit, try to relax."

Jackie turned to him. "That's what you call her?" she said. The choreographer shifted, absorbing his mistake. The name was not on the list of things he could share.

"It's fine," I told him. "I'm sorry we're wasting your time," I said to Jackie.

"You're not," she said. "He pays me by the hour."

I looked at my body in the mirror, then my body in the flesh, reflection and actual not quite matching up. I'd dressed in dark jeans, a blue slouchy sweater, the baggy sleeves hiding my arms. Underneath the fabric—the bruises, a map of all that happened between us.

A woman with a secret. A woman with a choice.

Looking at the choreographer, I brought my thumb and forefinger to my neck in a loose half circle. He tensed again and shook his head.

"No," he said.

"You said you would do what I wanted," I said.

"Rabbit."

"You said you wanted her to embody me," I said. I didn't recognize my voice, the woman sitting in the glass. She wanted to take something. She wanted to hurt. "You said you wanted to show me."

"No." He stepped back slightly away from me. "Not like this."

"Yes," I said, and the woman in the mirror took hold. "Just a little."

He exhaled, turning away from me, from Jackie, who looked openly confused.

"Are you sure?" he said.

I nodded.

He stepped forward as if to come close to me, then stopped, remaining on the other end of the room.

"Kneel," he said. I got on my knees on the floor, facing off with the woman in the mirror.

"Whoa," said Jackie.

"How do you feel?" he asked.

I closed my eyes, dropped down again. A word. "Humiliated," I said.

I could feel him across the room, all wound up and unhappy. *You're torturing him*, I thought, but I couldn't stop.

"Do you like it?" he asked.

"Yes." Each yes became another notch tighter around him.

"Why?"

I spoke softly. "Punishment."

"Get up," he said. "Stop." We'd agreed: no punishment.

I got back in the chair, body relaxing. Looking at him, I said, "There's no way this isn't humiliating for me."

He held my gaze. *You did this.* Then he turned away, desperate for a place to crawl off to. "Kneel," he said.

I got back down on my knees, my bones aching as they pressed into the floor. Closing my eyes, I waited, anticipation moving like breath across my neck. I felt him through all the air and space between us, tuning in and waiting for what he would say.

"Stop—get up," he said. I pushed up to my feet and stayed standing. "I can't, this was a mistake. I'm sorry, Jackie. You can bill the time. I'll see you at group rehearsal."

"That's fine," Jackie said, crossing the room toward the door. Her eyes met mine in the mirror. "I got a lot out of that anyway."

He shut the door behind her and leaned his forearms against it, bracing. Pressing the edge of a clenched fist on his forehead, he let out a long, slow breath.

As I watched him, the urge to punish finally relented. "I'm sorry," I said.

He shook his head. "No," he said. "It's my fault. I shouldn't have brought you into this."

He met me in the center of the room, wrapping his arms tight around me. I leaned my cheek into his chest. I'd failed. *Trust me*, he'd said, and I hadn't.

Letting me go, he settled slumped on the chair.

"I shouldn't have made it," he said. "The solo."

"Why did you, then?" I asked.

He rubbed his cheekbone, his jaw, embarrassed even though there was no one else in the room. "I think I want to share you, and then I can't," he said. I remembered what he'd said to me, the first time I'd visited the practice space. No one would see how we moved, together and alone.

"Like with the barista," I said, settling onto the ground at his feet. He continued to look away.

"Sort of," he said. "Sort of like that."

I slid between his knees, kissing his legs and wrapping my arm around his calf. "It's okay," I said, resting my cheek against his thigh. My reflection there, the woman gone now, just a sweet animal playing. "I'm yours. You can keep me."

He stroked my hair, then hunched his body over mine, kissing my ear. "When you say that," he said, "I don't think you realize how much it's the other way around."

I closed my eyes, feeling his mouth on my hair, the top ridge of my ear. "What are you trying to do with this solo, anyway?"

He breathed out, his ribs deflating near my head as he sat back up. "I'm not sure anymore," he said. "It keeps changing. I think I'd like to show you something new. About you. And me. This." He touched my arms. "Something that will let you be."

Pressed against him, my skin went cold. The email. The story.

Pulling away, I turned to look up at him. "I need to send you something," I said.

CHAPTER FIFTEEN

After dinner, he put on his glasses and sat on the couch, reading. I couldn't stand to sit next to him, so I got up and started rubbing down surfaces that were already clean, wetting and wiping the counter with lavender-scented spray. Every cough and shift drew my attention as I tried to decode his reaction.

Then, the slight *tink-tink* of his glasses folding. "Are you done?" I asked.

"Yes." His voice sounded wary.

"What did you think?" I asked, leaving the kitchen area to return to the living room.

"The movement is confusing," he said. "Is this supposed to be contemporary ballet or modern?"

I knew well enough not to ask, *What's the difference?*

"You can help me with that," I said. "What did you think?"

He closed the laptop, bracing his palms on the hard clamshell. "It's beautiful."

"But?" I supplied. I'd heard the *but* in his voice.

"It's cruel," he said. "The characters are cruel, and you're cruel to them."

His eyes, when he finally turned to me, looked tired and hurt. The skin around them twisted as if to shield the irises from damage. "Is that how you see us?" he asked.

"No," I said. "It's not. It really isn't."

He rubbed his face, the hurt showing his age. I kept talking. I needed to find new words to undo the ones I'd written down.

"I want it," I said. "What we do. It feels . . . wonderful." My feet felt stuck into the ground, like stakes. "And it confuses me."

"Do you think I'm bad for what we do?" he asked.

"No," I said.

"But you think *you're* bad."

He'd pinned me. I didn't answer.

"It's not to degrade you," he said. "Do you understand that? It's . . . I . . ."

He gripped his fists, his words faltering, and so I picked up the thread instead.

"What we do—I feel like it takes me out of me, if that makes sense," I said. "It brings me somewhere else. Another place I've never been."

I watched his response to each word, hoping I'd stumble onto the right one. *Please*, I thought, *oh please.* I would have done anything to soothe him.

"And I want it very badly," I continued. "But I've also spent my life trying to be me. So I don't understand why I want to stop being me so much. Why I want to stop being anything."

"I don't want you to stop being you," he said.

"I know that," I said. The words were wrong, the right ones weren't coming.

His face stayed blank, as if my speech had overwhelmed his systems. I wished I could sit down and touch the understanding into him, but my feet stayed rooted. The air in the room developed a new viscosity that kept our bodies apart.

"The story came from a time when I was trying to figure something out," I said. "When I wasn't . . . When I was being mean."

"Do you feel differently now?" he asked.

"Yes."

"Why?"

"You," I said. If I couldn't move toward him, then I'd throw words out like little life rafts, hoping one would reach him and keep us both from sinking.

"That's not enough," he said. "I want you to feel differently because of you."

I didn't know what he meant.

"Are you angry?" I asked.

"Of course not," he said. "I wouldn't be angry over this."

Our shared space grew dense with new fog. He looked away from me, staring at the table, his hands.

"Did your agent like it?" he asked.

"Yes," I said. "She wants to send it out."

"Good." He stood up, putting the laptop aside. He came to me and kissed the top of my head, perfunctory and dry. "She should."

And then he left the room to get ready for bed, alone.

I TOOK A late train back to Boston on Sunday, gliding into South Station through the dark. A rideshare home, the river, the bridge, all routine now.

During the train ride, I'd emailed the agent to send the story out, then closed my laptop and spent the rest of the ride staring out at the sea. *What have I done?* The choreographer's pain sank through me.

I opened my apartment door and found Annie sitting on the couch. Walking into the room felt familiar but strange, like putting on a favorite dress that suddenly failed to fit.

"Hey, stranger," she said, resting her laptop on the couch as she turned to me.

"I'm not a stranger," I said, dropping my keys on the mail table.

"I haven't seen you since, like, Wednesday." I'd taken Friday off of work to go down to New York early.

"That's just a few days, Annie," I said. I opened the fridge. No food of mine.

"I made some chicken," Annie said. "If you're hungry."

"Thanks. That's okay though," I said.

I went into my room and dumped my bag on the bed. Annie followed me in. "Is something wrong?" she said. "Did you guys fight?"

"No. Not exactly." I left my backpack by my desk. One of his scarves hung over my chair. I'd asked for it, for something that smelled like him. I picked up the edge, pinched the soft fabric between my fingers.

"I think I hurt him," I said.

"I'm sure you didn't," said Annie.

I saw his eyes, the pain. "I really did." I'd broken something, felt it crack.

My phone buzzed. *Back home yet, love?* he wrote.

Home. What did that mean now?

"Doesn't he hurt you all the time?" Annie said.

"No," I said, starting to text back. *I'm back in Somerville, if that's what you mean.* "That's different."

I kept texting. *Happy Birthday again*.

Immediate dots. He'd started typing back.

"Are you full-on dungeons and whips yet?"

"I'm not a joke," I said, staring at my phone. "My sex life isn't a cartoon."

I hope this doesn't make me too old for you now.

A beat of pleasure. At least he was flirting.

"C," Annie asked, "are you okay?"

"Of course I am," I said. "Why do you ask?"

"How else would I know?" she said. "You're always gone. Why are you always going to him?"

"We're together. Why shouldn't I?"

"Because you live here," she said.

Never, I wrote.

"This weekend, I met Esme's new girlfriend," she said. "In Boston. She really likes her, and you've never met."

"It was his birthday."

Thank you for coming to the city so much.

Hey. Boston is a city, too. I added the winking smiley face with the stuck-out tongue.

"And the weekend before?" she said.

"All we have are the weekends," I said. "What do you want, Annie?"

Puritans, he wrote.

"I want you to stop being so weird," she said. "It's like you don't even want to be here anymore."

I finally looked up. The skin of her cheeks blushed hot red. "I'm sorry," I said. "Do you want to go to Trash Night at the Brattle? I can text Esme."

"Sure," she said. "That would be fun."

Hardly, I typed into my phone without looking.

"You and him," Annie said, looking at my phone. "What's going on?"

I'll come up next weekend, he wrote. *I'll see you in the mountains.* Relief. I'd see him again soon. I'd touch him.

"Isn't it obvious."

"You're, like, lost."

"No," I said. "I'm just in love."

She looked stricken, slapped. "Oh," she said. "I didn't know that."

"I love him," I repeated. The words glowed, printed all over my skin.

Her face turned in on itself, absorbing the hurt, the shock. "That's great," she said. "I'm happy for you, C. You've got a fancy New York boyfriend."

I waited. She probably had more to say.

"Glad you're back."

"Thanks," I said. "I should get ready for bed."

"Okay." She left my room. I turned back to my phone. *I can't wait.*

Chapter Sixteen

The next weekend, I didn't even tell Annie my plans, just got in my car on Friday and drove. Early darkness, the traffic, then the house waiting for me at the other end.

He had dinner ready. He wrapped me up in his smell, his arms. But then, in bed, something different. A gentle care and hesitation, his touch light on me.

"What's wrong?" I asked. Bare, we stayed huddled under the covers for warmth. "Is this because of the story?"

"Yes, I suppose," he said, touching my cheek.

"Please, don't be mad."

"I'm not mad." He wove his fingers through my hair, cupping the back of my head. "I want you to feel good. I can't do it if it makes you feel bad."

"Can't it make me feel both?" My hands pressed against his ribs so I could feel the air moving through him.

"I know," he said. "But you—I don't want to damage you."

"I'm not damaged."

"I didn't say that right." I pulled myself flush against him, wrapping my arms under his shoulders so my head fit under his chin.

"I just can't do it." He took a hunk of my hair and buried his face in it. "Not right now."

"You can't do this to me," I said. "You can't change me and then send us back, leave me alone."

"I don't want to change you." His arms curled as if to protect me, like my body had become something delicate and fragile. "I love you."

I pressed my face into his neck, his jaw, feeling the light stubble against my skin. The night at the theater, my early pursuit of him. Not like me. Even Annie said. Some fresh and subtle gear had driven my life into his.

"It doesn't matter what you want," I said. I rose, surfacing, my mouth soft against his. "I'm different. I've changed."

AFTERWARD, DRIVING BACK into the city, I crossed the river. While I'd been gone, the ice had broken, letting the dark water flow. We'd returned to spring without me noticing. Back to the melt, the thaw.

AFTER WORK ON Tuesday, I walked over to the Bolshevik bar on Mass Ave to meet Annie and Esme. I got there first, before anyone except two hardcore barflies playing darts by the back. Settling down with my book, I ordered a drink and waited.

Esme appeared first. "Ez, I love your hair," I said, touching the short sweep of her new asymmetrical bob.

"Thank you," she said, smiling. "Lily likes it, too." The new girlfriend, a research scientist who did something intimidating with genes.

She got her own drink and took her place at the stool by my side.

"Do we know what's on tonight?" Esme asked.

"Not yet, I don't think." The theater didn't announce the movie for Trash Night until the last possible moment.

The middle-aged woman in a black cap landed a bulls-eye. She clutched her hands into fists, crowing with glee.

"How's everything?" Esme asked, looking at my hands, my face. Not my arms. "With him."

I sipped my beer. "I love him," I said. "Did I tell you that?"

"I had a feeling."

"But I think . . . Remember—" I touched my own arm. She nodded. "I think I misunderstood something and now—" I stopped. Another sip, restarting. "He won't do it anymore."

She had a talent, really, for not reacting.

"And how does that make you feel?"

I didn't look at her but watched the skinny man take his turn, throwing and missing, the dart landing in the plywood behind the board. "A little lost," I admitted.

Annie came in, unwrapping the layers she wore for cold-weather biking. Her cheeks were bright red, her body radiating cold. "Oh my god," she said. "What did I miss? What were you talking about?"

"Esme's new hair," I said. "Doesn't it look great?"

Annie smiled. "Yeah," she said. "You look cool, Ez. Whose idea was it?"

"I've been thinking about it for months," Esme said. "But Lily pushed me to try it."

"That's great," Annie said. "I hope it won't be a pain to grow out."

We finished our drinks and moved on to the movie theater where we stuffed ourselves with popcorn. The movie was a coming-of-age story about rollerblading and climate change. We howled at the wooden dialogue, throwing kernels at the screen.

Afterward, Esme couldn't linger, leaving to start the long subway ride back to JP. Annie and I were left alone.

She pushed her bike on the sidewalk, walking with me back to our apartment.

"Did you have fun?" I asked.

"Of course," she said. "I love Trash Night."

We passed the window of a sex shop. FEMALE-OWNED SINCE 1972! The bare white mannequins wore leather straps and bright red feathers.

My sex life isn't a cartoon.

"Are you hanging out with Buzz Cut–Lip Ring this weekend?" I said.

"No," Annie said. "She's kind of boring, I realized."

"Oh. I didn't know that."

"Don't worry," she said. "I'll be occupied."

A buzz. My phone. I didn't look. "I know," I said. "I'm not worried about that."

"Clearly."

We got back to the apartment. Annie went straight to her bedroom.

I made some tea and lingered on the couch, checking my phone. A picture of one of Neil's experimental whole-wheat boules, more texts from the choreographer. An essay about the photographer Graciela Iturbide and a picture of his local bodega cat, a tuxedo lump stretched over a block of Irish Spring.

I scrolled through the essay, but didn't really read, listening to Annie in her bedroom, her thump and quiet tread.

A COUPLE OF weekends later, I stayed in Somerville on Friday night to go to a friend's goodbye party. Because she was moving to Sweden, we ate meatballs, elk-shaped pasta, and drank small, cold glasses of vodka.

Annie and I went out onto the chilly roof-deck to smoke a spliff. "Congrats on your story," Annie said. That morning, a journal had accepted it for publication. I'd texted Annie about it at work, then put the phone in Airplane Mode so I wouldn't be waiting for her response.

"Thanks," I said.

"They rejected one of mine last month."

"Oh, really?"

"Yeah. So yours must be really good."

She lit the spliff then passed it to me so we swapped spit. "Why didn't you give it to me to read?" she said. "Before you gave it to your agent."

"I don't know," I said, exhaling a puff. "Everything kind of happened fast."

Her lips pressed tight together. "And you're out of town all the time again," she said.

I held the spliff out, passing it back without looking at her. "Yes," I said. "I am."

She sucked on the end, the cherry glowing. Before us stretched the flat plain of Cambridge leading to the river, the city on the other side. "C," she said, "I have to talk to you about something."

The leveled seriousness of her voice sobered me up. "What?" I said. "What is it?"

The spliff had formed an end of ash. She tapped it out over the edge of the balcony. "It's about your relationship," she said.

My back tensed, the wings of my shoulder blades drawing together like armor.

"I'm glad you're in love and all. I really am. But I just don't feel very comfortable with it."

She could have pushed me to the ground. She could have sucked up all my air.

"I need you to help me feel better," she said.

"Really," I said. "What do you mean?"

"I need you to work a little more, so I can understand it," she said. "Otherwise, it just doesn't feel good to me."

I didn't look at her. I tried to swallow, but everything in my throat had gotten gummed up, dried and thick. "What do you have in mind?"

Annie didn't hear that my voice had changed, had turned dense and solid and sharp. "Maybe you could set up some one-on-one time between me and him," she said. "Like he could come here and we could spend a day together. So I can get a better picture of what this is all about."

I could still feel my heartbeat, but the air turned clearer, as if a new sense had turned on. "I don't think that's going to work."

"If you want me to feel better about you and him, then you need to do this."

I thought, but did not say, *What if I don't care?*

Finally, I looked at her. "Why can't you just trust me?" I said.

She reached out, touching my hair as she passed back the spliff. "I love you," she said. "You know that. That's what this is about. You and him, what you do. I wouldn't put up with it. I wouldn't put up with the things you put up with."

My lungs pinched, full of something solid and sharp like ice. I stubbed out the spliff even though it wasn't finished. "I'm going home," I said.

"What? Why?"

"It's snowy," I said, although it wasn't. "And I've got a drive tomorrow. But you stay."

"C—" Annie called, but I was already heading back inside, saying my goodbyes.

I heard her come in late. Pouring water, drinking in the kitchen. My light was still on, but she didn't knock, didn't say my name.

When I woke, I still felt the hush of her sleep through the rooms. I packed my bag quickly and headed out the door.

An hour into the drive, the crying hit me, a blend of rage and grief. I cried so hard I couldn't see and pulled over at a rest stop, the car settling in front of an orange Gulf sign. *Fuck her*, I thought. *Goddamnit, fuck her.*

I'd told Annie to trust me, but did I trust myself? What did I want at the end of all this, and who would I become to take it?

I closed my eyes, still clutching the steering wheel at three and nine like I'd been taught. I breathed deep into my belly, my chest. *Sink*, I thought, and down I went into my core. I looked for who I was, who I planned to be. My crying quieted as I found the pulse, the throb. I listened and held. I found the frequency of belief.

HIS CAR STOOD parked outside the house. I let myself in with my key. A quiet filled the rooms, like the building was holding its breath. "Hello?" I called. I checked the living room, the bedroom.

I found him by the pond, dressed in warm active wear and working through new movement. In motion, his beauty brimmed with purpose, arcing and reaching, limbs cutting and taking command of the open space. He radiated, both human and otherworldly.

He landed on one leg, balancing. I stood on the other side of the glass, not breathing. The first time I ever saw him dancing.

Twisting, he turned upward, his torso unfurling as his chest and neck opened to the sun. I pushed aside the door, stepping out onto the deck. "Hello," I said. "I'm here."

AS WE HAD sex that afternoon, I tried to goad him, to incite him, but he pushed me back. "No, Rabbit," he said.

"Please," I said. We were curled on our sides facing each other, my hands swimming toward him even as he lightly rebuffed them.

"Not like that," he said. "I'm just not in that particular mood."

He lifted me on top of him and fucked me sweetly, but the whole time I felt my body and his, separate and sustained. Back in myself, my form, alone.

After dinner, I sat for a while with my notebook at the kitchen table. Every word I put down seemed out of place. Annoyed, I realized that my mother's work was all about this. How these little objects could seem so particular and precise but often miss their targets.

"Congratulations on the acceptance," the choreographer said, passing me with his mug of tea.

"Thanks."

He stopped. "You don't seem all that happy. Is it because of what I said?"

"Partly."

"It doesn't mean it's not a good story."

I didn't reply. *I wouldn't put up with the things you put up with.*

"Is something wrong?" he asked. "Did something else happen?"

I inhaled, sank down again to find the pulse and throb, a comfort and a push. "No," I said, "Nothing happened. I'm coming to bed soon."

He came close, kissing the top of my head as I breathed in the chamomile steam. Then he left, settling down with *The Gorgeous Nothings*.

I closed my notebooks, got out *Bluets* and followed him to bed.

"I'm going to leave Boston," I told him as I pulled the covers over my legs. "I'm going to move."

He didn't act surprised. "When did you decide this?"

"Today," I said. "During the drive."

But I couldn't quite say all of it. Instead I turned to the book, stared at it like I could bore myself into the start of a paragraph.

He watched me pretend to read. "We could live here most of the year," he said. "Have more space."

I let the book go and turned to him.

"I don't know," I said. "I know more people in New York."

I felt the space between us ease. We'd docked, arrived. "When does your lease end?" he asked.

"June."

He opened his book, flipping a page. "Wonderful," he said.

CHAPTER SEVENTEEN

Annie and I did not speak of the choreographer again. The conference took up all her time. Late hours at the office, phone calls, folding name tags and sticking them into lanyard pockets until two in the morning. I found her passed out with all the welcome packets at our kitchen table. My anger eased and I brewed her a cup of tea.

I also had to get ready for my presentation. I hadn't taught a class since English Composition at UMass. I picked too many readings, loaded my presentation with too many slides. How did I think I would say all of this in the allotted time?

"Should I come up for it?" asked the choreographer over the phone.

"No," I said. I flipped through my packet. Did I expect people to read through all of this? "It's going to be very esoteric. A craft talk, not a reading."

"Are you nervous?" he asked.

"Incredibly."

"Don't be," he said. "Just be your brilliant self."

The morning of my session, I got dressed and ate my breakfast of oatmeal and chia seeds, the choreographer having finally converted me to the weird little globules. "Don't wear that," Annie said, looking at my blue velvet dress. Her own dress was tight and floral with big sleeves. "Wear a suit jacket and pants," she said as she put on a big dangly earring, "so people will take you seriously."

"You're wearing a dress," I pointed out.

"I'm just handing out lanyards," she said. "You're one of the stars."

I changed into black jeans and a suit jacket, but kept my hair half-up, half-down, putting on lots of dark eyeliner. Annie gathered all her hair into a single elegant puff.

"You look great," I told her. The dress hugged her body so tightly I could see her tendons flex.

"So do you," she said. "Let's go." She ordered a rideshare to take us to the grand hotel just off the Common.

Together, we passed through the spinning doors into a glossy lobby lit by crystal chandeliers. I remembered the awe I'd felt at the dance festival that summer. The glow and art of the dancers, their bodies, their beauty brought out into the open air. I didn't realize that Annie lived in a world where writers shone as well, except our glamour came from our casings, vaulted tunnels of language and money and prestige. Our fortresses turned brighter, bigger, all while our grubby bodies burrowed deeper into the ground.

Annie found my green lanyard. She looped it around my neck and tucked it under my hair. "Go get them," she said, and sent me off into the hordes.

Off the grand ballrooms, the hotel turned into a series of mazelike hallways, several different historic buildings put together through questionable renovation. They were dense with the ponderous huddles of conference-goers struggling past each other like cattle on the way to the next feeding pen. Annie had given me a map with my room circled in blue ink, but I couldn't tell what side was supposed to be up. Eventually, I asked one of the brightly T-shirted volunteers to point me in the right direction.

I found it, a long, narrow room darkened by heavy blinds. I turned them open and found myself staring at a cement air shaft. Back to closed, then, the blinds shutting out the concrete. Then I fussed with the stack of handouts at the back, the pads of paper embossed with the hotel's name, and sucked on one of the bountiful candy mints. Stress-sweating under my suit jacket, I wished I'd worn the dress.

Six people came to my room, scattering from the middle to the back. They watched as another volunteer helped me attach my laptop to the projector and focus the lens on the screen. For some reason, I'd picked the famous painting of Saturn eating his son for my first image.

"Hi, everyone," I said at the start of the allotted time. I said my name, where I'd gone to school. "I'm the author of *The Anderson Kid* from Three Lemurs Press. You can't really buy it anywhere, but I have some copies with me for sale."

A man stood up. "Sorry," he said. "I'm in the wrong room."

I didn't say anything, watching him go.

"So," I said, "I'm here to talk about experimental prose forms."

The session went surprisingly well, with people flipping through the readings and pulling out strong lines, though at one point I did start ranting that "Freytag's pyramid is a capitalist project." But one middle-aged woman even bought my book.

"I'm obsessed with Centralia," she said. "Ever since I heard a podcast about it."

"Yes, that is the inspiration," I replied.

My session over and still high off the adrenaline, I surged back into the masses.

"Hey!" Annie found me in the hall. "How'd it go?"

"It went okay," I said. Through an open door, I spied an essayist who had recently rocketed from failure to fame, graying and looking stunned in his T-shirt. Many members of the standing-room-only crowd clutched his most recent book, their faces open and awed.

"Great. I wish I could have gone," Annie said, her hand on my shoulder. "I have to get back to the front desk, but see you tonight for the after-party."

I snuck into the famous essayist's session, listening to his talk. I tried to note what seemed like sage advice on my phone, but only caught about every tenth word. *Follow the Shadow! The heart of the heart of the sentence.* Everyone looked so hopeful. Everyone wanted something.

I went to a couple of other sessions. "Using Sports to Get Through Writer's Block," "What Does Revision Really Mean?" I didn't follow the content, but standing in rooms full of intense attention set off the odd ring in my body, the loosening I'd begun to recognize as a sign of work. Zoned out, I followed problems in my writing through to solutions, to ideas for new stories.

Another T-shirted volunteer pointed me to the presenter breakroom where plates of mini bagels and baked goods had been left out for snacking. I camped out on the couch, jotting down notes for a story with one hand while eating a small cheesecake with the other. In front of me, the sky turned orange, deep pinks shifting above the Common.

At the end of the conference, I left the break room to find Annie. She was on the hotel's mezzanine, stacking boxes of unused name tag sleeves and information packets. The muscles of her arms strained as she carried the boxes across the room.

"Hey," I said, stepping inside. "Do you need any help?"

She turned to me, her face breaking open into a smile. "No," she said. She put the box on top of the stack and shoved them all to the edge of the table. "I think I can leave this for the interns."

We found our coats in the rows of racks and stopped to check our makeup in the hotel bathroom. Then we left the building, walking around the park to the official after-party at a major donor's house. Only presenters and the invited editors and agents were permitted.

"Did you have a good time?" she asked. "Learn anything new?"

"Sure," I said, sticking my hands in my pockets. Cold again, Boston weather always threatening to drift back into winter. "Learned plenty." We passed the duck ponds, the water illuminated by the weak streetlights.

Annie's phone directed us down Newbury Street. "Is this party taking place at a shoe store?" I asked.

"Just wait," she said. "You're not going to believe it."

We ended up in front of a stone doorway, the rest of the building covered by scaffolding. The door seemed simple, made from heavy wood and beveled glass.

Annie tried the doorknob. Open. She stepped inside, her back straight, and I followed, immediately stunned by the vaulted marble foyer centered around a tall crystal chandelier. "What the hell?" I said. At the back, carved stairs wound to the upper reaches, the walls filled with gilded nooks and wood paneling. I'd never been to a private residence built on the scale of a public building. A table full of long-stemmed glasses, wine bottles, and liquor blocked the entrance to the stairs, and on the landing above us perched a trio of live musicians playing music into the air.

"I know," Annie said, hooking her arm around mine. "The owners are actually named the 'Richmans.' You should check out the basement. They had a pub shipped over from Ireland."

She steered me toward the drinks table, giving me wine, then more wine, as if I were not drunk enough on the heady opulence. She introduced me to people, then sent me out on my own to rotate through the gallerylike rooms. I blurted to the famous essayist that I loved his book as we both waited for gin and tonics, and I talked earnestly at the director of a prestigious MFA program despite already having an MFA. I took a picture of a stuffed giraffe in the library and sent it to the choreographer. *Who the hell are these people*, he texted back, *and are they interested in modern dance?*

I found the food mound in the glorious kitchen and ate some crackers and cheese and carrot sticks, trying to snack my way back to sobriety.

"You're Annie's roommate, right?" said a man I recognized as one of Annie's coworkers. Maybe a writing instructor at the nonprofit, I wasn't quite sure. "I remember you from her birthday party last year."

"I am," I said, swallowing the food on my plate. I quickly brushed my mouth for crumbs.

He pointed at my name tag. Most of the partygoers still had their name tags on, having forgotten we were no longer at an official function. "I didn't realize you were a writer, too," he said. The lanyards were color coded, the green ropes indicating my position.

"I am," I said. "I have a story coming out soon." I told him the name of the journal.

"That's fantastic," he said. "That's a really good journal."

A hot flash of pride flushed up my spine. "Thank you," I said.

The alcohol had loosened my tongue, and I kept on going. Who represented me, my book, my presentation, heady with the unfamiliar pleasure of talking at length about myself. The man nodded, encouraging. I mentioned the Maine residency, the two weeks there.

"I've been meaning to apply," he said. "I heard it's lovely."

"It's great," I said. "I met my partner there. He lives in New York. I'm moving soon, actually. To be with him."

Saying it out loud, it didn't sound so bad. Like something people did.

"That's great. That'll be great for you," he said. Then he added, "Does Annie know?"

"Not yet," I said. "Don't tell her."

He winked. "Your secret's safe with me."

"There you are." Annie walked in. Her arm looped through mine. "Having a good chat?"

"She's telling me all about her news," the man said. Annie looked briefly confused.

"My story that's coming out," I said.

She smiled, beaming. "I know, right?" she said. "They rejected a story of mine two months ago, so hers must be really good."

A man in a suit and a purple lanyard—I was unsure what that meant—clinked a fork against the edge of an empty wineglass. "Speech!" he shouted. "Time for speeches, everyone. Let's all head back into the foyer for the speech."

The man winked at me again, glancing at Annie. "Good luck," he said.

"Ready to go?" Annie asked. I stuffed a last cracker and gruyere into my mouth, then went with everyone out into the main hall.

The executive director stood on the staircase. "Thank you all for another wonderful weekend, another wonderful year," he said. "Over these last three days, we've heard stories, we've gained wisdom, we've come together over our love of words."

He looked at Annie, some special cue, and she let go of my arm and started moving through the crowd.

"But I want to give some special thanks to the wonderful Annie Michaels." And Annie slid her narrow body behind the wine table, stepping up to join him on the stairs above us. "This was her first year taking on the conference. Don't you all think she did a marvelous job?"

We clapped, we whistled. She beamed above us, perfect in her dress, her bun. My chest lit up with bursts of old love. I clapped until the palms of my hands hurt, cheering for her, for Annie, my lovely, golden friend.

The speeches finished, and we returned to mingling.

"Aren't you having a great time?" Annie said, coming to me and taking my arm again.

"I am," I said.

"I'm so glad I could bring you," she said. "C'mon, let me show you the bathroom."

We walked through the kitchen to another, more humble set of stairs leading to the quiet of the upper floors.

"This is as big as our apartment," I said, following her inside and shutting the door. There was one toilet, one massive tub, rococo furniture filling the rest of the room as if it were another public lounging space. "Wouldn't this get moldy?" I said, sitting on the edge of the plush chair.

"Who knows?" Annie said, standing in front of the giant gilt mirror. She zipped open her makeup bag and dug out a tube of mascara.

"Thanks for bringing me on."

"Of course," she said, brushing one eye. "See what a good time you have when you stay in Boston?"

My heart picked up. *Not the time, not the time,* but the words came up anyway.

"Annie," I said, "I have to tell you something."

She looked away from the mirror, mascara brush still in hand. "What?"

"I'm moving," I said. "I'm moving to New York."

I thought the words would turn into stone. Instead, they ignited, a massive explosion.

"What?" she said. "Why?"

"You know why," I said.

Her lip curled. "Him."

"Yes," I said. "Him."

She jammed the mascara brush back into its tube. "Why couldn't he move here?"

"His company," I said. "His career."

"What about *your* career?"

"I'm a *writer,*" I said. "It's *New York.*"

"Boston is a great place to be a writer," she said. "Did you not just hear that speech?"

"Annie," I said, "you know why I have to go. I can't do long distance anymore. It's been a year." With some surprise, I realized I was right. "I want to be there with him."

She pulled the mascara wand back out and turned to the mirror to apply another coat. "What are you going to do there?" she said, voice full of bite. "Who do you even know?"

"I'll figure it out," I said. "All my UMass friends live there."

"Like that shitty guy Ian?"

"And Vera and Rita."

She smiled at herself in the mirror. "All your straight friends."

My grip tightened on the edge of the plush couch. "Annie," I said, "watch it."

She jammed the wand back in, screwing it tight. "You have no idea," she said, and her face in the mirror turned sharp, lips smiling to show the length and breadth of her bite. "Do you know how ridiculous you look? Running around after your rich boyfriend?"

A flash, a thought. "Do I look better running around after my rich best friend?"

She threw the mascara back in her bag. "We're not like that."

"Are you sure?"

Now she faced me. "Do you know what you're doing? What you're giving up? The risk?"

My shoulders relaxed back, chest out, a strange calm settling over me. "I think I'm risking just enough."

"You're being an idiot."

The calm began to heat, to boil. "Annie," I said.

"Don't turn this on me. On us." Her nose flared, her lip curled. "You need to take a good look at you. At what you've become."

"And what's that?"

214

"Some man's little woman."

I stood. "Fuck you."

"You're making a huge fucking mistake."

"And you're being a judgmental bitch."

She turned red to the roots of her blonde hair. "Fuck you," she said. She stuffed her makeup bag back into her purse and left, slamming the bathroom door.

CHAPTER EIGHTEEN

We found a way to live in the same apartment without ever seeing each other, our charged magnetic forces keeping us apart. We roved and raged through the small rooms, silently seething.

One day we ran into each other in the kitchen, both of us in pajamas. "Are you seriously not going to apologize for calling me a judgmental bitch?" she said.

"Are you going to apologize for judging me bitchily?" I said.

The red face again. "No," she said. "You're such an idiot. You're such a goddamn fool."

"I'M SO SORRY, my love," the choreographer said over the phone.

I sat on my bed staring at the piles of clothes on my floor, trying to figure out what to take, what to give away. On the other side of the apartment, Annie smoldered, a volcano of silent feeling.

"Is there anything I can do?"

"No," I said. "I can't think of a thing."

"Do you still want to move?"

"Yes."

"Do you want to come down early?" he asked. "I mean, if it's too much to stay there with her."

I dropped back on my pillows, the phone in my hand.

"No," I said. "I should stay and try to see this through."

"She can't stay in her room forever."

I got up and crossed my room, standing in the doorway. The apartment stretched like a sea, a battlefield, Annie's door a wall on the other side. "You don't know," I told him. "You don't know Annie."

"I WANT YOU to know," Esme said over coffee, "that I think she's being totally out of line."

"Thanks, Ez," I said, lifting my mug with both hands. I wasn't sleeping well. I imagined Annie wasn't, either, the two of us electrifying the apartment with our joint anger.

"She's just freaked out," Esme said.

"I know it's a lot," I said. "I know it's a big move."

Esme stirred her coffee, pouring in a packet of brown raw sugar. She'd always been the level one between us. Our steady ship.

"It's not that," Esme said. "It's not just him. It's what's happening to all of us."

"What do you mean?" I said.

She put her mug down. For the first time, I noticed a few gray hairs peppering the short side of her bob. Later, I'd brush out my braid and find one of my own.

"We're changing," she said.

★ ★ ★

THE EDITOR OF the journal sent me a file full of Track Changes. I didn't open it. I couldn't stand it, not on top of everything. I still blamed the story for the shift between me and the choreographer. His tender, concerned care made me feel somehow weaker than what we'd done before.

"I feel weird, getting ready to move when things don't feel totally right," I told him once, on a wet, gray day in the Berkshires. A damp chill kept us huddled under the covers. Speaking to him beneath the blankets made me feel vulnerable and new.

"I know," he said. "But it's not that things are wrong."

"I don't understand," I said.

His fingers brushed my shoulders, my back, as if testing their strength and integrity.

"I wish I were better at telling you," he said.

I'd been so afraid of his power over me. Now I'd been tilted too far in the wrong direction, a different kind of trap. Would I move only to be lost in a cage of my own fragility?

He kissed my collarbones, my neck. "We'll figure it out," he said. "Do you trust me?"

I took his face into my hands. The texture of his skin on mine, the sharp pleasure of our difference. "Yes," I said. "I do. I trust you."

MY ALARM WENT off at five A.M.

I made a full pot of coffee, drinking it down as I sat at my desk putting words in front of each other. Mostly, though, I watched the day spread out across the world, a wonder in itself. On the other side of the apartment, Annie dressed. Brushing hair, pulling on pants, a sweater. She made even the sound of cloth on skin seem angry.

She left earlier than usual now, avoiding me. Once the apartment door had closed on her, I ventured from my room for more coffee as I got ready for work.

Down the Somerville hill to Cambridge, following the path to my cubicle. Piles of discarded furniture blocked the sidewalk. Trash day. Moving day. Garbage bags bulged with the unwanted, the things that hadn't made it on to the next life.

With the school year wrapping up. I should have been more free at work, but a professor came in, asking me to rescan a book. "The first one's a little crooked," he said. "Try to get them straight this time. Otherwise, it's too hard to read."

He left the volume on my desk. Four hundred pages on the economic history of Hungary. He hadn't explained why he couldn't just read the book itself. I started up the old scanner, the alien sound of its electronic hum.

As the machine droned, I went to my personal email and finally opened the story.

Light spilled over the lip of the stage, illuminating the director's expression. Her attention held the dancer like ropes, a gentle pull leading her until she filled with a power greater than the sum of them.

The comments were mostly about pronoun ambiguity. Annoying, I realized now, that I hadn't bothered to give anyone a name.

The dancer's feet bled, cracks bursting between toes, her body pushed beyond enduring. But she wouldn't stop turning, not now. She'd circle and twist. She'd linger, she'd spin, sheltered by the director's certainty.

I addressed the comments, I sent it back, and then I closed the file and dragged it to the trash can icon on the desktop.

Maybe I still felt heady from the fumes of the fight, living inside my anger. Maybe it was just the gender change. But looking at the story now, I could see a different read. In some ways, it could have been about me and Annie.

MY PARENTS CAME up to New York one morning to meet the choreographer over brunch. He wanted to book someplace impressive, but I warned him not to dazzle them. We ended up at a kosher vegan dim sum place that made a convincing gluten shrimp, sharing a huge circular table with a family of four that never looked up from their phones.

He still brought my mother a large bouquet of hothouse gladiolas. She gave what she called her "faculty meeting" smile, an unpleasant, narrow grin. "Thank you," she said, placing them on the ground by her chair.

Sitting together, I had to admit that it looked like my parents were hanging out with their friend and had included their daughter for some reason. My parents sat between us, twin walls again, so I couldn't grip the choreographer's hand and use the pressure to tell him to slow down or shut up. His nervous tendency to talk too much would put off my parents as it had put me off in Maine.

"So," my dad said, "you run a dance company."

"Yes," said the choreographer, "but I'm not like a starving artist or anything. I can take care of your daughter."

"She doesn't need taking care of," my dad replied.

"Of course." I smiled a little, watching the choreographer's usual presentation unravel. "But I could if she wanted. Which she doesn't. She really doesn't."

My dad made eye contact with my mom, passing a silent comment, then grabbed the last shumai from the bamboo steamer.

"Also," the choreographer said, "I've convinced her to move to New York."

I glared. *Not now!*

My parents forgot about the choreographer, turning to me. "Honey, is that true?" my mother said.

"Yes," I said. "When my lease is up."

"That's fantastic," she said. "Boston is a terrible city."

"You'll be so much closer," said my dad. Their pleasure washed over the table like cool, artificial air.

"Oh, but Annie," my mother said. "What's Annie going to do?"

The choreographer watched, as if his gaze were a net that could catch me. I didn't flinch.

"Esme's taking my spot," I said. "She's going to be fine."

My mother reached for one of the fake-shrimp dumplings. "Good," she said.

"Have you figured out work?" my father said. "My colleague mentioned they're hiring a new coordinator over at Brooklyn College."

I glared at the choreographer to keep him from speaking. "No," I said. "I might try to find something that has more to do with writing."

"Just don't teach," my mother said. "The market's abusive."

"I know, I know," I said. My mother had recently joined the faculty union and now filled our family emails with rants on the appalling state of academia.

She reached over and squeezed my wrist. "I'll be glad to have you closer, honey."

"And we have a guest room, so you could visit whenever," the choreographer added.

The air cut off, back to stuffy heat. Even I could not follow the shifting expressions of my parents' silent communication. The general movement seemed first to the choreographer, a quick conference with each other, then back at me, my mother taking the lead. "You're going to move in with him?" she said.

I put on my best imitation of my mother. "Yes," I said.

"Maybe only at first," said the choreographer. "Whatever she wants."

He really needed to stop saying that.

The rest of the meal continued rather stressfully, with the choreographer finally remembering to praise my mother's work. The move backfired, though, as she grilled him on his interpretation until he descended into gibberish.

We decided to go together to the Vija Celmins show at the Met Breuer. The choreographer offered to carry the flowers for my mother, but she held on, hugging them to her chest. "I've got them, thanks." Then, five minutes later, she said, "Nate, can you give me a hand here," and my father carried them until we checked our belongings at the gallery.

I stood in front of one of the dark ocean scenes, absorbed in the graphite water. The choreographer came up behind me and whispered, "How do you think it's going?"

My parents stood together in front of one of the deserts. "I don't get it," said my dad.

"Nate, she did these all in pencil."

"These are *drawings*?"

"I think it's going well," I said.

After the museum, we said farewell to my parents, wishing them a safe drive back to Philly.

Returning to the apartment, I took off all my clothes and got on all fours with the pink tie around my neck, hoping, but the choreographer just sort of fidgeted with it in his hands.

"You know I was lying about you finding your own place, right?" He pulled on the tie, and I felt a slight twinge of excitement blended with irritation. "I'd like you to stay here. For good."

I arched my back, annoyed cow pose. "I really don't want to talk about my parents right now," I said.

He dropped the tie, standing up. "You can get up," he told me.

I got to my feet, pulling off the tie and draping it over the back of the chair. *So much for that.* As I tugged on sweatpants and a T-shirt, the choreographer paced around the apartment looking at the guest bedroom, the walls.

"Do you think it went well?" he asked.

I'd heard my father mutter "I'm not calling that old fucker 'son,'" as he got into the car. "Sure," I said, opening the fridge. The choreographer kept buying fancy bottles of Gerolsteiner, but I stuck to the plain, generic-brand seltzer. "I mean, I think they're a bit baffled. But I wouldn't worry too much about it."

He stood in the doorway of the guest room, peeking back at it. "I was thinking, when you move, we should maybe redo some things. If it'll make you feel more . . . at home."

"Okay," I said. I put some bread into the toaster oven and found the salami he'd learned to keep supplied for me.

"Like, we could redo the spare bedroom. With a Murphy bed or something, so the rest of the time it could be your office."

"An office," I repeated.

"So you could take up the floor and the walls, like in your studio in Maine."

I'd forgotten that we'd let everyone into our workspaces, that he'd seen the insane rats' nest way I preferred to work. "I forgot that you saw that," I said. "It's funny. It feels so long ago."

"Would you like that?"

"I would." The toaster went off. I occupied myself with spreading hummus and arranging salami slices.

"I'm overwhelming you."

"A little," I admitted.

I wanted him to come and hug me from behind, but he stayed by the door. We felt more apart now, more talking, less touching, receding from our bodies into words.

"I just want you to feel comfortable here," he said. "Equal."

I finished setting up my snack, then looked at the table, the light fixtures, the windows with their views of the sun and the trees. "That's going to be really hard," I said.

"Does it have to be?"

I shifted a salami slice with my nail, perfecting the line. "Did you ever feel equal with your ex-wife?" I said.

He took a moment. He wanted a different answer. "No," he said. "Never."

"Can you imagine how much harder it is for me? To be in that position?"

"Yes," he said. "Or, no. But that doesn't mean I don't want to try."

How I wished he would kiss me on the head. "Okay," I said, looking at him. "I appreciate it. We'll try."

He finally did come over then, squeezing my shoulder. "I'm glad," he said. "And then, you can tell me what to read for the next time I have to talk to your mother."

Chapter Nineteen

I sold my car, no need for two. Sold my bed, my dresser, all my temporary things. What I'd take with me turned out to be pitiful, filling a single moving van that my brother came up to help me drive. All the while Annie continued to avoid me, her door closed in stubborn, silent rebellion.

On my last night, I stayed up late taping boxes, reluctant to go sleep on the couch. Annie came in, drunk and stoned and crying. She started kicking the boxes with her bare feet, bruising her toes.

"Annie," I said, "what are you doing?"

She collapsed on the floor, her spine and shoulders slumped. Her face had blotched up and gone red with crying. My anger shifted at the sight of her, so small and sad. "How could you do this to me? How could you leave me?" she said. "We were supposed to have a beautiful friendship."

"We still can," I said, but she shook her head.

"No," she said. "You're different. You've changed."

"It's 'both and,' Annie," I said. "I'm me, and I've changed."

But her head continued to shake as she pushed herself up from the floor. "No," she said. "I don't know you. You're a stranger to me now."

IN THE MORNING, Annie's door was shut. It stayed shut as Neil and I carried boxes down into the moving van. Finally, the last one was gone, the room echoing and bare. I wiped down the windowsills and swept up the hair and dust from the floor.

"Annie," I called from the kitchen, "I'm leaving."

Nothing. I theatrically dropped my keys onto the counter. "I'm leaving my keys for Esme."

The door stayed shut. "Annie," I said. "Are you seriously not going to say goodbye?"

I waited. And waited.

Finally, I left, shutting the apartment door and leaving everything behind.

I WOKE UP in the choreographer's bed. Our bed. I sat up and stared, not sure what to do.

He opened his eyes. "Hello, my love," he said.

I ran my fingers through his hair. "Hello, my life," I said.

He frowned. "Are you doing that thing where you're quoting something again?"

"Yes," I said. "I'll tell you about it, one day."

We got up and made breakfast. My move coincided with the lead-up to the company's new season, so he didn't have a lot of time. "I still miss this, you know," I said, holding up the pink tie as I looked for a shirt.

He kissed my temple. "I know," he said. "We'll talk about it more after the premiere."

Then he left. My days stood open like windows, like doors, each one holding so much time. Not since Maine had I had this level of freedom.

I unpacked my things. He'd paid someone to install a wall of shelves in the spare bedroom, now my office. My books didn't even fill half of them. Would I be here long enough to see them full?

The white spindle-legged desk I'd pulled from a curb in Amherst went by the window, my blue bookshelf beside it. On top of the shelf, I put the print of the rotund plant-women, the picture of me and Esme and Annie. I watered the new aloe on the windowsill, set up the lucky rocks I'd found in Maine. On the wall, a fresh printout of *10 Rules for Students and Teachers*. I took a picture and sent it to Annie. *New writing spot*, I wrote.

It wasn't even lunchtime yet. I wrote in my notebook, I looked for jobs, applied to be a part-time assistant editor at a literary magazine. Before, the pay would have been impossible, but now it wasn't, now that I lived with the choreographer.

I checked my phone. No response from Annie.

I went for a walk, came back and took a shower, still stealing the choreographer's thyme shampoo. Looking at my sudsy hands, I wondered if this was what true adulthood meant. No more communal thinking, no shared thrill. My own body, my actions, a new power I couldn't articulate, but also bereft, alone.

Later, I met the choreographer for dinner at a Thai restaurant near the rehearsal space. "Did you hear from her?" he asked.

I scooped some green curry over my rice. "No."

"I'm sorry, darling."

I smashed a corner of the white rice cake. "It's fine," I said.

He watched me, not touching his food. "Do you blame me?" he asked.

I pushed around a green snap pea. "Sometimes I try," I said. "But it doesn't help. It doesn't make it any better."

I spooned up the snap pea with some rice, putting it in my mouth.

"I'm sure she'll respond," he said.

I swallowed, not saying anything.

"Do you want to see a movie tonight?" he asked.

I ate another mouthful. I knew the curry was full of flavor, but none of it reached me. "Sure," I said. "That sounds good."

"SHE'S STILL MAD, I think," Esme said over the phone. I paced the apartment, looking out at the windows, the trees. "I don't know. I wish I had better news for you."

"It's fine," I said, touching the leaf of one of the new snake plants I'd bought at the grocery store.

"I miss you," Esme said.

"I miss you, too."

"Is everything good with him?" she said. "New York sounds super dreamy."

"It is," I said. "You should come down to visit."

"I will."

She held a silence that stretched into meaning.

"I have to warn you," Esme added, "I think she's writing something about you."

My throat tightened, my feet freezing. I stopped in front of one of the small gilt mirrors the choreographer kept around out of superstition. He thought they deflected envy. Warped and speckled, the antique glass took in the world to return a marked and different version.

I saw Annie grabbing my arm, touching my bruises. I saw her studying, taking pieces of me. She'd build from what she found and show her construction to the world. A line of cause and reasoning, a dare and maybe also damning.

But all she had of me was the same thing as the glass, a strong but still inaccurate reflection.

How I was perceived mattered, this was true. But it wasn't all of me. Beneath the surface lived something large and uncontained. No matter what I said, what play I took part in, no one had that. Not the choreographer. Not Annie.

"Fine," I said. "Let her write whatever she wants."

Chapter Twenty

The morning of the premiere, I woke up curled on my side, the choreographer's body wrapped around mine. "Are you awake?" I said.

"Mm-hmm," he breathed into my neck.

I rolled over to look at him, his loveliness shining through the exhaustion and the stress. I kissed his half-asleep mouth, his face. "Good morning," I said. "Are you ready?"

He opened his eyes, aligned straight with mine. "No," he said. "I'm not."

I put out the cashew yogurt even though I knew he wouldn't eat. "Are you nervous?" I asked.

"As always," he said, pouring coffee.

I grabbed my regular yogurt, some coffee as well, and sat down at the table.

"What about you?" he said. "Isn't today your interview?"

"No," I said. "They pushed it off until Monday. I'm meeting up with Vera and Rita."

"Say hello to them for me," he said.

I smiled.

"Say hello to Jackie," I said.

He matched my grin and kissed me. "Sure."

We dressed and he gathered up his things. "I'll stop by before to get ready, to get you," he said.

"Good," I said. I kissed him on the mouth. "What am I supposed to say before this? Am I supposed to say 'Break a leg?'"

"That works," he said, and then he was gone.

I wrote a little, then took the long train ride to meet Vera and Rita in Bushwick for an indulgent Friday brunch. We lingered over *cafecitos*, fans turning in the airy Cuban restaurant.

"I'm so happy you're here," Rita said. "I kind of can't believe you moved."

"I can," said Vera, cutting into a pillowy poached egg. "I saw the apartment."

I sliced into my breakfast empanada. "It's a little surreal," I said. "But a relief. I couldn't take any more Amtrak sandwiches."

"When are you going to invite us over?" Rita asked.

I sipped my coffee, my fourth or maybe sixth of the day. "Soon," I said. "We're changing the apartment a little bit. To make it more me, kind of."

"I'm so jealous," Vera said.

"I wouldn't be," I said. "It's really complicated."

"A hot rich guy loves you," Vera said. "What's complicated about that?"

A little woman.

"A lot," I said.

"Is this because Ian called you a housewife?" said Rita.

The chunk of bread and cheese stuck in my throat. "He told you that?" I said.

"Vera did," Rita said. I looked at Vera, who hid behind her coffee mug. "Look, Ian's a jealous little shit. Do you actually love this guy?"

"Yes," I said. No hesitation, not anymore. "I do."

"Then fuck Ian," Rita said. "You're not doing anything wrong."

All of your straight friends.

"Thanks, Rita," I said.

We took some coffee to go and went for a long walk, eventually reaching the water's edge. The ferries powered by, the occasional tugboat heading off to guide a container ship. On the other side of the water, the city stretched and glistened.

"How's your dissertation going?" I asked Rita.

"It's good," she said. "I mean, it's horrible. I worked so hard to get here and now I don't want to do it."

"I can't finish this screenplay, either," Vera said. "I don't know, I'm just not connecting with it."

I thought if they had worked with econ professors for three years, they might feel a little differently.

"But you guys can come next weekend, right?" I asked. The journal planned to launch the new issue at a Brooklyn bookstore. Now that I was conveniently local, they'd asked if I would read.

"Of course," Vera said, half hugging me with one arm. "Can't wait to hear it."

She let me go, and we stood staring at the water. My dance story. And now here I was, living with the choreographer.

We stopped in a bookstore before I took the train back. The random items by the cash register, the children's books and greeting cards. I walked alone into the fiction section, scanning the alphabet until I found my place on the shelf and pressed my finger to the crack. Passing the *M*s, I paused to do the same for Annie.

The subway took an age to spit me back in the choreographer's neighborhood. I let myself into the apartment and closed myself in the office. For a while, I worked on my application for Yaddo, where the choreographer and I both planned to apply, and then, when I was sick of it, opened the edited draft of my story to figure out what I would read.

While writing, I thought I'd made the dancer weak, but as I scrolled through, I saw how the world pivoted around her. The other characters reacted, deflected, her smooth passivity sparking something in them and also, I now knew, inside of me. I'd gone through her still expansion and emerged different on the other side. *No one*, I'd written, *understood the dancer's power, how it took everything to reach the edge and let go.*

Odd how a piece of your own writing can read strange to you, a beacon into parts unknown.

I heard the choreographer's footsteps, his key. I closed the document.

Stepping out of the office, I met him in the common space. "Can you eat anything before?" I asked.

"No," he said, running his hand through his hair. "I don't think so."

"Are they ready? The dancers."

"Probably," he said. "I think I've lost all perspective."

He showered, shaved, the minimal tasks needed to amplify his beauty. I pulled on a black cowl-neck dress and tights, brushing out my long hair and pinning it back from my face with giant bobby pins. Gold earrings, a bit of makeup, my dark austerity matching his. This was my role for tonight, a sort of living accessory.

He went out to the fire escape to smoke his second cigarette of the year. I watched him, a spectator again for a moment. The bedroom window framed the long hunch of his body, his legs outstretched, his arms still in motion. The cigarette up, the hand smoothing his hair. I'd put him back at a remove, the bright god I couldn't quite touch. I wished I could take stills of him, eerie and perfect in the golden hour.

He came back through the window, and I met him in the living room, hugging him. "Are you nervous?" I asked. He rested his chin on the top of my head.

"I don't know if I'm more afraid of them, or you," he said.

"The solo," I said, keeping the side of my face pressed against his chest. His heart there, steady.

"Yes," he said. "We'll see."

He ordered a car to take us to the theater. We didn't talk on the ride. He held my hand, his fingers woven through mine. The streets cut through the city like canyons, and I looked up from my place on the ground to the tops of the buildings, the windows catching the last of the day.

The marquee of the theater announced the name of the show. MOVES FOR PREDATOR AND PREY. He kept his hand on the back of my neck, and we walked together through the door.

Once inside, the flurry descended, people in black appearing from doors and hallways, all *Welcome, sir, how's your evening?* Back in his world. His assistant swept him off for a last-minute check on the dancers, the costumes, leaving me alone in the lobby.

A young man in black, an usher and probably also a dancer, came to get me. "Ma'am," he said. "I'll show you where you and the director will be sitting.

I felt my mouth tighten, the ghost of my mother's faculty-meeting smile. "Thank you," I said, and followed him through the aisles of the empty theater to my seat. Front and center. The stage crew were still adjusting the lights, testing the sound.

The airy silence of the building spooked me. I didn't want to just scroll through my phone, sitting in the middle of everything like a prop for people to gawk at, so I got up and left the theater, circling the block. I stood for too long outside the window of a deli, staring at strangers. The air had cooled since the sun went down, and I hugged my upper arms, rubbing the goosebumps through the fabric.

When I returned, a different usher grabbed my wrist. "Miss, I need to see your ticket."

"Yo," another usher called, "that's the director's wife or something."

His hand sprung open, releasing me. "Oh my god," he said, "I'm sorry."

"It's okay." I tugged my sleeve back in place. "It's really fine."

Now the seats were full, some people already sitting, others standing, clustered and talking. No one noticed me, a lone young woman. They were too busy looking at each other, taking in their finery.

The choreographer still had not returned. I took my seat, quiet and anonymous, until he reappeared, pulling me up. "Ready for the wolves?" he said. I put on my smile and we got ready for the rounds, except we didn't move, the rounds coming to us.

"My dear," Ron said, taking my hands and kissing both of my cheeks. "So glad you've left the Puritans and moved down here with us."

"Me too," I told him.

Franny appeared. "Hello, Wellesley," she said, and I smiled through the knot of pain. Annie and I in our graduation gowns. Annie and I lounging on a bright green lawn.

The ex-wife approached. I took her smooth, dry hand. "Lovely to see you again," I said, smiling at her much-richer husband.

Her face remained poised. "Charmed," she said. "Can't wait to see what he's spun up for you."

I hugged, I smiled, I kissed. *My partner, my partner, my partner.*

And then the lights flickered throughout the theater. Time to settle down. We took our seats, wrapped together in the dark.

The curtain opened on the full company, the ensemble performance I'd watched in rehearsal more than a year ago. *A lifetime*, I thought. Before, I never would have noticed, but now I saw the millimeters of new tension in their muscles, anxiety and self-awareness. I understood then the tragedy that I'd never see how they danced without the pressure of performance. Still, the nerves made them glitter, a different kind of beauty.

Enthralled by their movements, I almost forgot, but then the rest of the dancers fled the stage, leaving Jackie curled on the ground.

She had a moment before the music started, and from my seat in the front row I could look straight into her eyes. Her chest heaved in the secret dancer way, struggling for oxygen while also showing little effort. It would be her last New York season before the hip injury that ended her career. *I'm sorry*, I thought at her, even though I had no idea what I was sorry for. If I hadn't been so drawn to her during that first show in Boston, I didn't know if I would be here now, dressed up in the choreographer's life.

The music was slow, heavy and ponderous, allowing her movement to take full stage. She didn't dance the way she did in the ensemble, the trio. She'd dropped the control, not quite in charge of how she commanded and steered the space.

If I'd properly studied the language of dance, maybe I could list out the moves she'd made, the lines and gestures, what they meant to other dancers. Maybe I'd have the words to place what she did to me, the way she'd rattled my core. But even after all these years, I've never really learned.

I watched her body rise as if propelled by a force outside herself, and my heart lifted with her, my body reflected. *Oh no*, I thought, my veins opening, my skin thinning, pinned like an insect to my seat but also up there, open and on display.

She let go, she merged, not a woman dancing but dance taking the form of a woman in order to be born. The spin of her arms, her legs were not movement, not energy, but great feeling, like love. She took all the love I had for him and all the love he had for me and she made it into something frightening. *To serve.* The words filled my throat, needing to be screamed. That's what our life would be, the purpose behind the breaking. I thought I'd served him all this time, but really he served me. The tie, the solo. All to figure out what I wanted and to give. All to take the two of us and merge us into one.

I won't survive this, I thought.

And the serving terrified me. So I broke it. That I could tell a man to take his love and smash it into the ground, and have him do it, again and again, until my body blossomed into something built by the two of us.

I won't get through it.

And at the end, she turned her back to all of us, that marvelous back that had so captivated me. The spotlight shone down on her like liquid silver. My body by the lake, about to jump. My body by the dock, disappearing. The woman in the mirror, in all the mirrors, chasing my body around.

I focused so hard on the strength of her spine that I felt myself dissolving, my internal pillars crumbling. A woman cruel and wonderful. So small and wild and determined to survive.

The music crested. A knot of tension, then release, her body breaking open and free. And with that freedom she fell, she melted, letting go into the ground.

The lights cut, plunging us in darkness, the crashing sound of applause filling the open space. My throat closed, I couldn't breathe, choked by the blood flowing through my own body. *I won't survive this.* And then I was out of my seat, up the aisle and running.

The stage door swung shut, cutting off the sound. My lungs tightened, gasping. I didn't make it past the lobby, collapsing on the floor against the wall. Did I need to cry? I felt all dried up inside, the air in front of me fogging. All the rooms he'd found inside of me broke and flooded, the flow and change unceasing.

The stage door opened. "Caroline?" he said. He saw me on the ground, and the air between us pulsed. "Rabbit." He knelt in front of me, grabbing my hands, his cheek pressed to my leg. "Are you okay?"

I felt the wall return to my back, the solid floor below me. I stared into his face and watched as the air turned clear.

"My love," he said, brushing my hair, my cheek.

I pressed my face further into his palm. *Bring me back*, I thought, *return me.*

"What's wrong?"

I reached out, my fingers in his hair, touching his face. "Nothing," I said, my throat thick and strange. "Nothing's wrong at all."

The understanding breathed between us, quiet at first before stirring with new life.

Taking his hand, I put it around my neck, an animal stepping willingly into a trap. "Whose am I?" I asked. "Who do I belong to?"

I felt his body ripple, the shadow flashed, and he gripped my neck in a light, hugging squeeze. "Mine," he said. "You belong to me."

"And we're not going to pretend any differently, are we?" I said.

"No." And he kissed me hard as if to bruise my lips, my fingers around the back of his head. Then he stood, taking my hand. He pulled me up into my life, into our life together, where I would inscribe each book, *For Joshua, who gave me everything.*

And the stage doors swung shut behind us.

ACKNOWLEDGMENTS

The best part!

Thanks so much to my brilliant agent Kate Johnson for believing in this book, and dream editor Callie Garnett for giving me the guidance and perspective needed to bring *Little Rabbit* home. And thanks to Akshaya Iyer, Nicole Jarvis, Patti Ratchford, Rosie Mahorter, and the whole team at Bloomsbury for giving *LR* a gorgeous face, catching my millions of errors, getting the word out, and all the hard work involved in sending a book into the world.

Thank you to Sam Allingham, Julia Bosson, Che Yeun, Liza St. James, and Larissa Pahomov for the eyes, advice, and conversation, and for making what is a solitary practice much less lonely.

Thanks to VCCA, VSC, Ragdale, and Ucross for giving me shelter as I figured my way to this book, and to all the other artists I met there for the inspiration. And thanks to Lighthouse Works, for holding my place in the midst of a pandemic and providing a safe habor to figure out what's next. Also, thanks to the MassMoCA Assets for Artists Program and the Mass Cultural Council. Special thanks to Bethany Arts Community—without my time at BAC, I never would have thought to write about dance.

Thanks to the Free Library of Philadelphia and the Cambridge Public Library, for the books.

Thanks to Don Lee and Max Apple, for the years of guidance. And thanks to Sheila Heti and my fellow workshop participants for helping me find the play in writing again.

Thanks to Jessamine Chan for sharing your tips, spreadsheets, and support. And thanks to Ling Ma for the Tarot readings and Sanaë Lemoine, who I'm excited to keep reading for many years to come.

To my parents, who are not allowed to read this book. To John and Sara, who are also not allowed to read this book. Benjy—I guess you can read it.

And, of course, to Matt.

A NOTE ON THE AUTHOR

Alyssa Songsiridej is an editor at Electric Literature. Her fiction has appeared in *StoryQuarterly*, the *Indiana Review*, *The Offing*, and *Columbia: A Journal of Literature and Art*, and has been supported by Yaddo, the Ucross Foundation, the Ragdale Foundation, the Vermont Studio Center, the Virginia Center for Creative Arts, and the Massachusetts Cultural Council. *Little Rabbit* is her first novel. She lives in Philadelphia.